NO LONGER PROPERTY OF
anythink LIBRARIES /
RANGEVIEW LIBRARY DISTRICT

D1442301

STONE ARCH BOOKS
a capstone imprint

STONE ARCH BOOKS™

Published in 2013
A Capstone Imprint
1710 Roe Crest Drive
North Mankato, MN 56003
www.capstonepub.com

Originally published by DC Comics in the U.S. in
single magazine form as Tiny Titans #5.
Copyright © 2013 DC Comics. All Rights Reserved.

DC Comics
1700 Broadway, New York, NY 10019
A Warner Bros. Entertainment Company

No part of this publication may be reproduced in whole or in
part, or stored in a retrieval system, or transmitted in any
form or by any means, electronic, mechanical, photocopying,
recording, or otherwise, without written permission.

Cataloging-in-Publication Data is available at the Library of
Congress website:
ISBN: 978-1-4342-4696-7 (library binding)

Summary: The Tiny Titans East invade the Sidekick City
Elementary playground! Plus, more Tiny Titans adventures!

STONE ARCH BOOKS

Ashley C. Andersen Zantop *Publisher*
Michael Dahl *Editorial Director*
Donald Lemke & Alison Deering *Editors*
Heather Kindseth *Creative Director*
Hilary Wacholz *Designer*
Kathy McColley *Production Specialist*

DC COMICS

Jann Jones *Original U.S. Editor*
Stephanie Buscema *U.S. Assistant Editor*

Printed in the United States of America,
in North Mankato, Minnesota.
052016   009770R

tiny titans

Meet Tiny Titans East!

By Eisner Winners
Art Baltazar & Franco

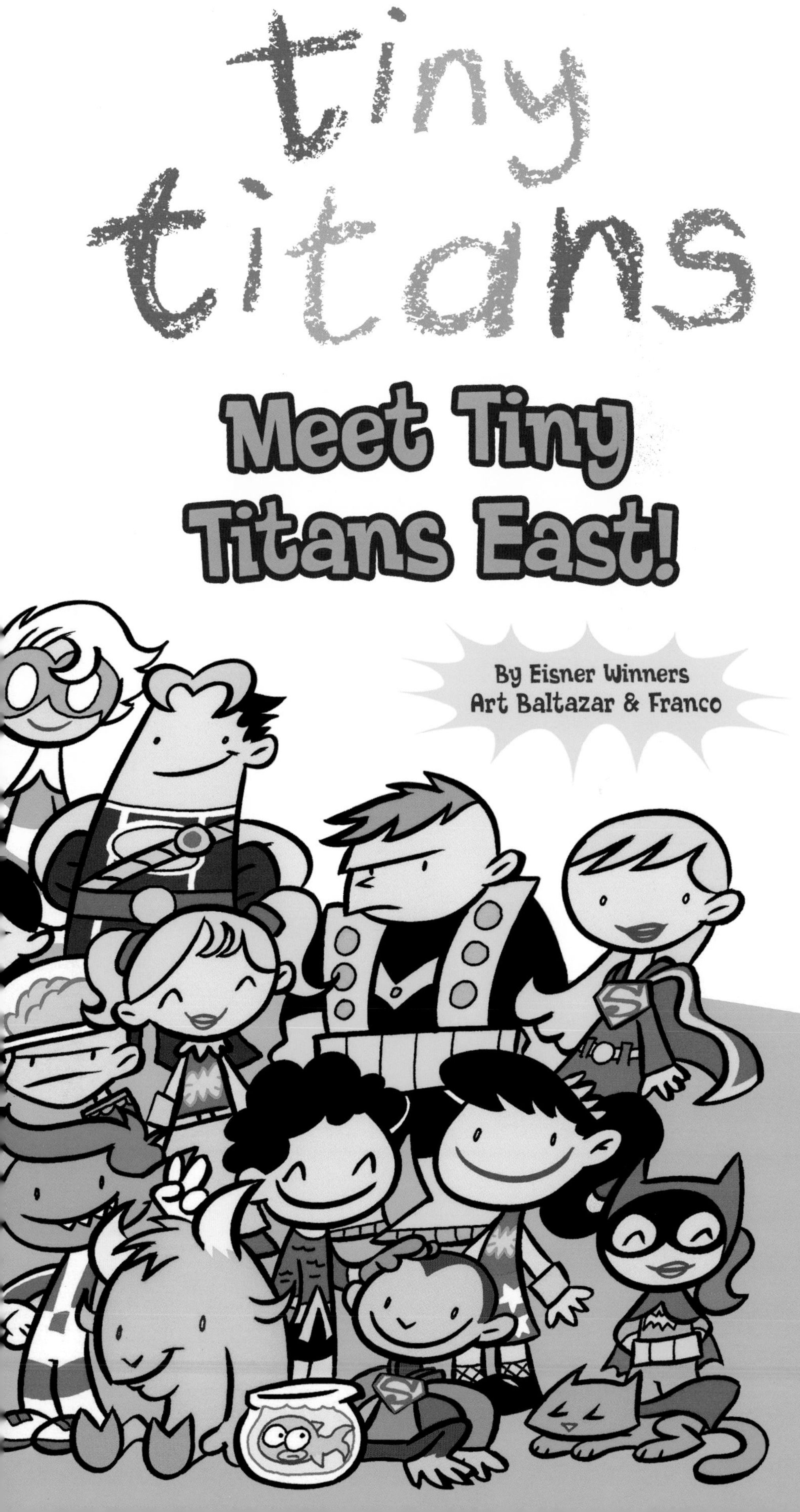

tiny titans

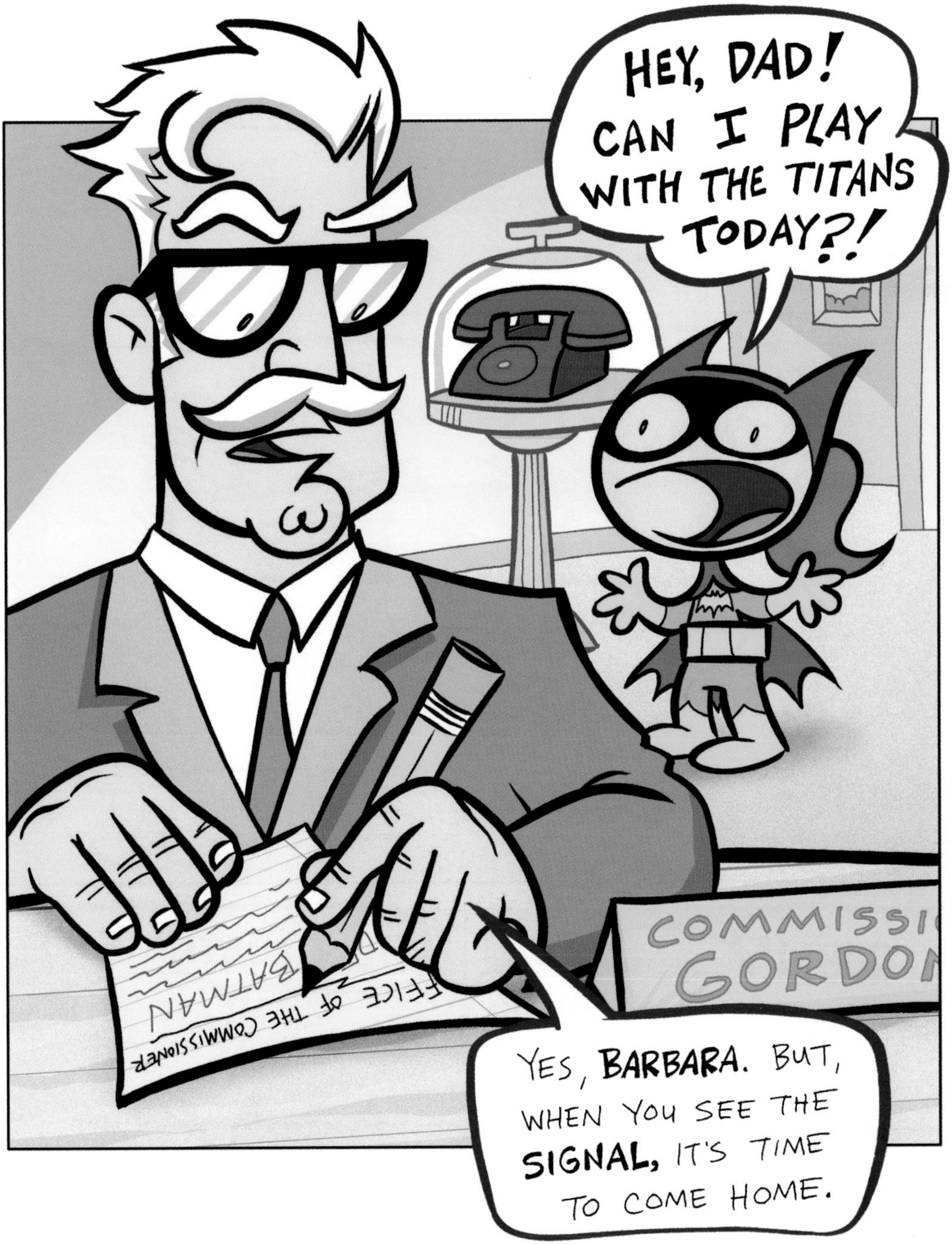
HEY, DAD! CAN I PLAY WITH THE TITANS TODAY?!
YES, BARBARA. BUT, WHEN YOU SEE THE SIGNAL, IT'S TIME TO COME HOME.

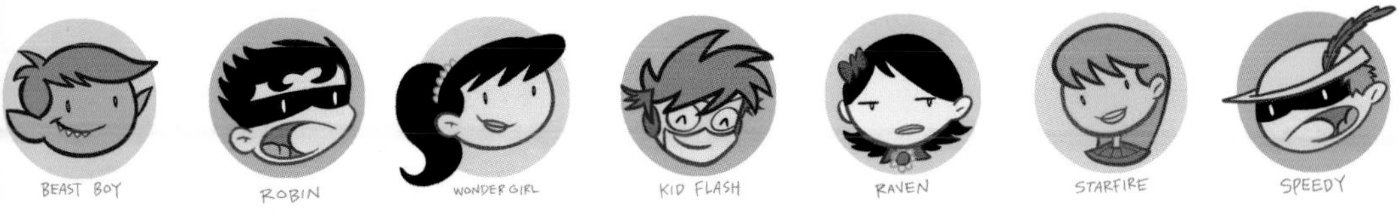
BEAST BOY
ROBIN
WONDER GIRL
KID FLASH
RAVEN
STARFIRE
SPEEDY

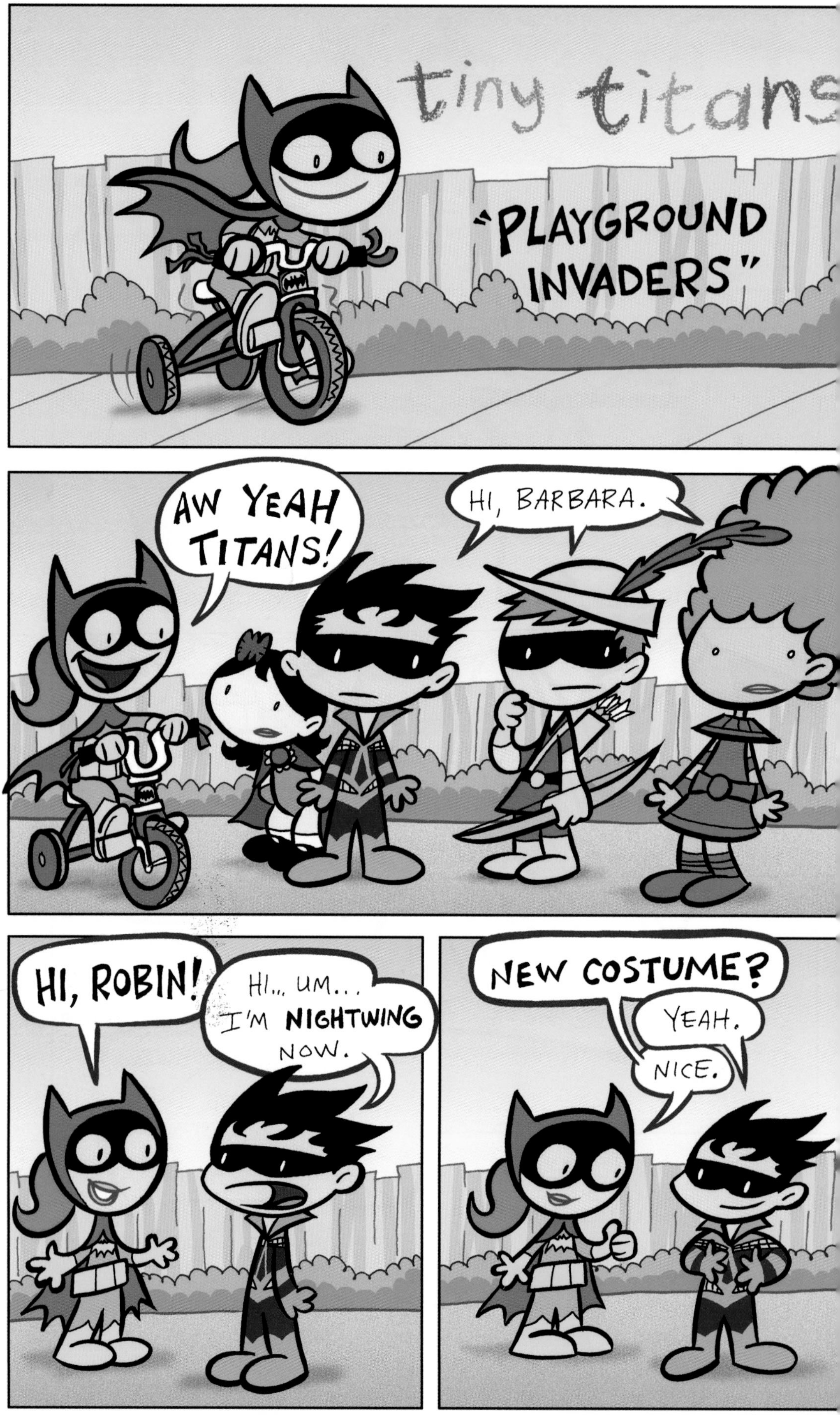
tiny titans
"PLAYGROUND INVADERS"
AW YEAH TITANS!
HI, BARBARA.
HI, ROBIN!
HI... UM... I'M NIGHTWING NOW.
NEW COSTUME?
YEAH.
NICE.

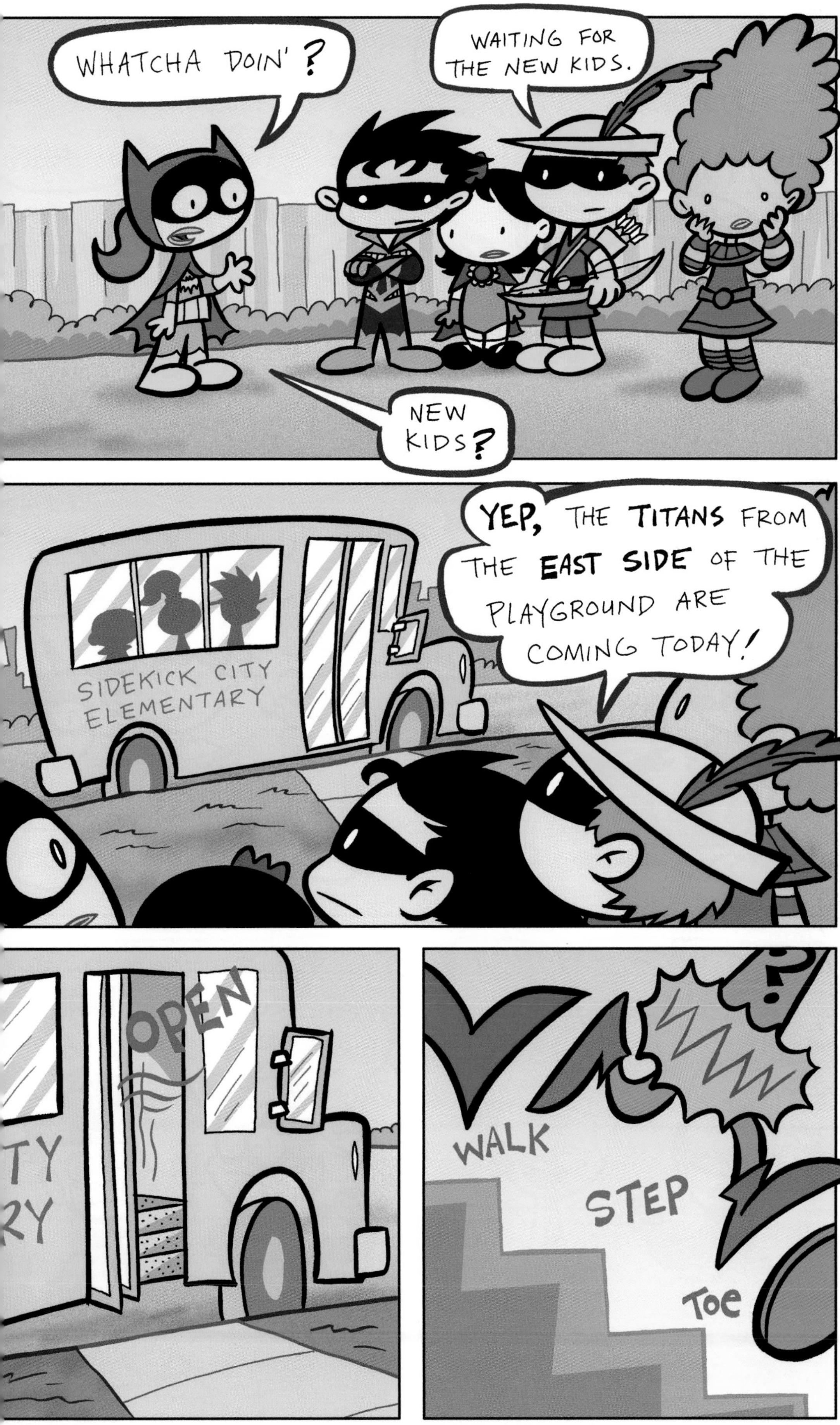
WHATCHA DOIN'?
WAITING FOR THE NEW KIDS.
NEW KIDS?
YEP, THE TITANS FROM THE EAST SIDE OF THE PLAYGROUND ARE COMING TODAY!
SIDEKICK CITY ELEMENTARY
OPEN
WALK
STEP
TOE

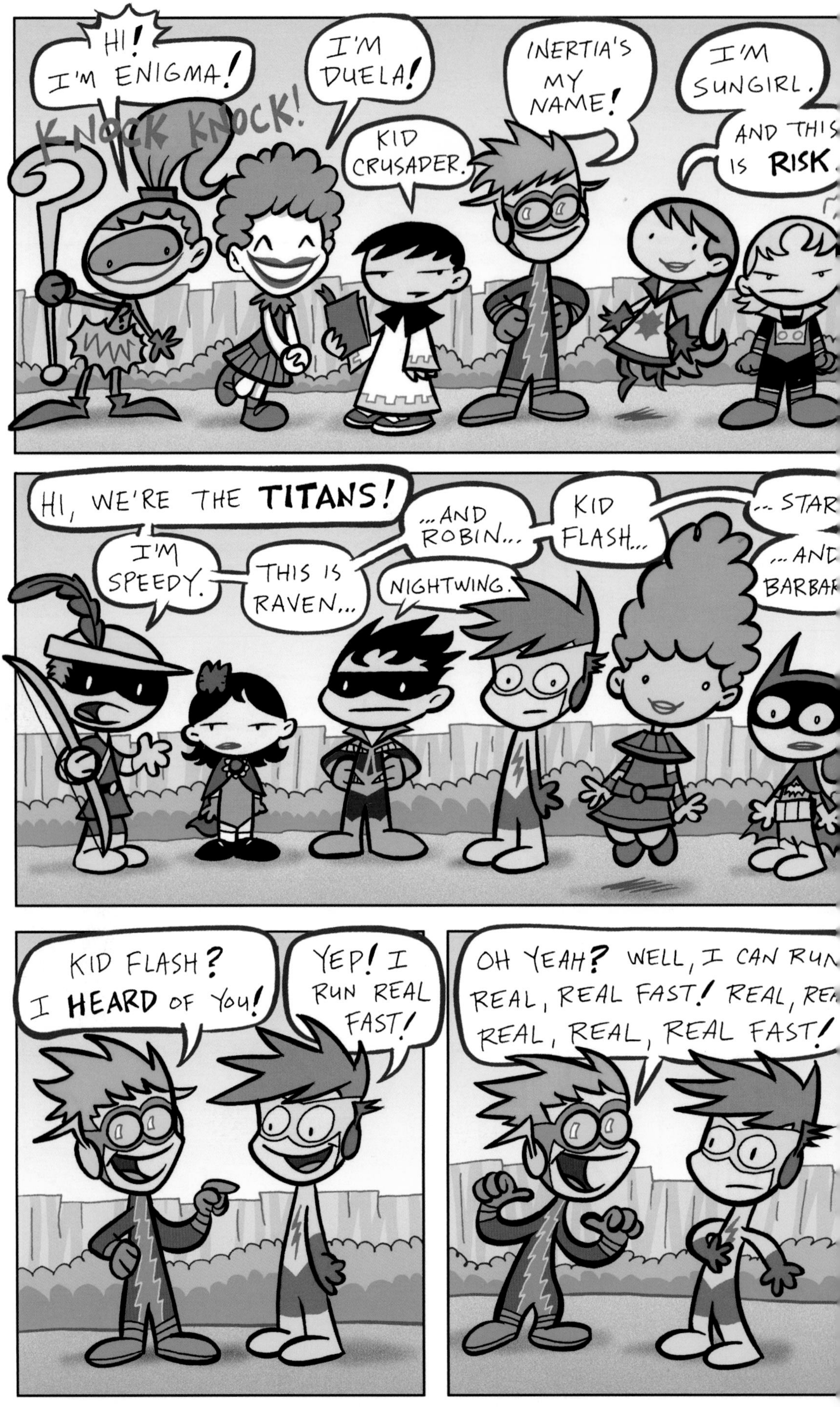

HI! I'M ENIGMA!
KNOCK KNOCK!
I'M DUELA!
KID CRUSADER.
INERTIA'S MY NAME!
I'M SUNGIRL.
AND THIS IS RISK.
HI, WE'RE THE TITANS!
I'M SPEEDY.
THIS IS RAVEN...
...AND ROBIN...
NIGHTWING.
KID FLASH...
...STAR
...AND BARBAR
KID FLASH? I HEARD OF YOU!
YEP! I RUN REAL FAST!
OH YEAH? WELL, I CAN RUN REAL, REAL FAST! REAL, RE
REAL, REAL, REAL FAST!

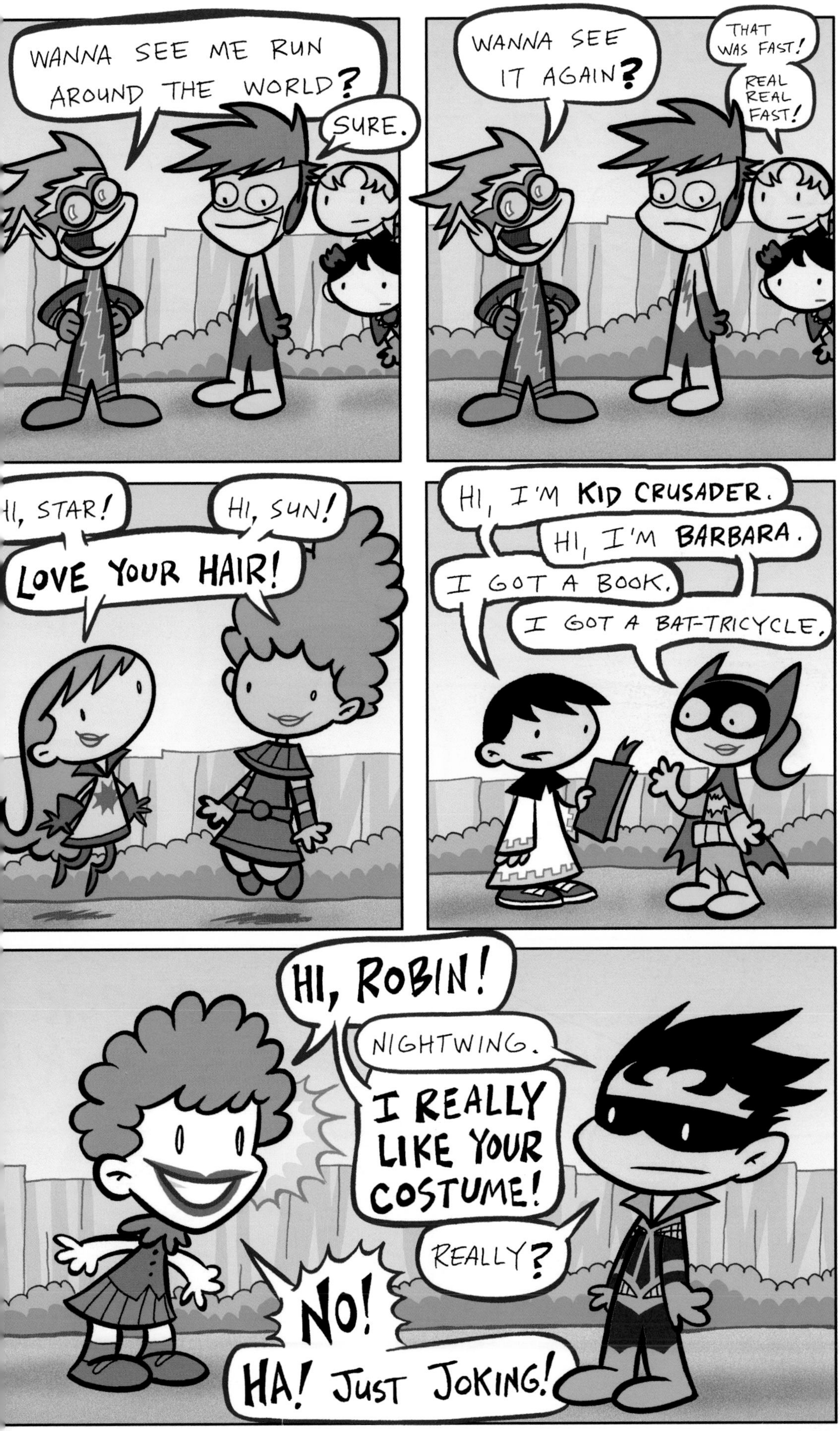

WANNA SEE ME RUN AROUND THE WORLD?
SURE.
WANNA SEE IT AGAIN?
THAT WAS FAST!
REAL REAL FAST!
HI, STAR!
HI, SUN!
LOVE YOUR HAIR!
HI, I'M KID CRUSADER.
HI, I'M BARBARA.
I GOT A BOOK.
I GOT A BAT-TRICYCLE.
HI, ROBIN!
NIGHTWING.
I REALLY LIKE YOUR COSTUME!
REALLY?
NO!
HA! JUST JOKING!

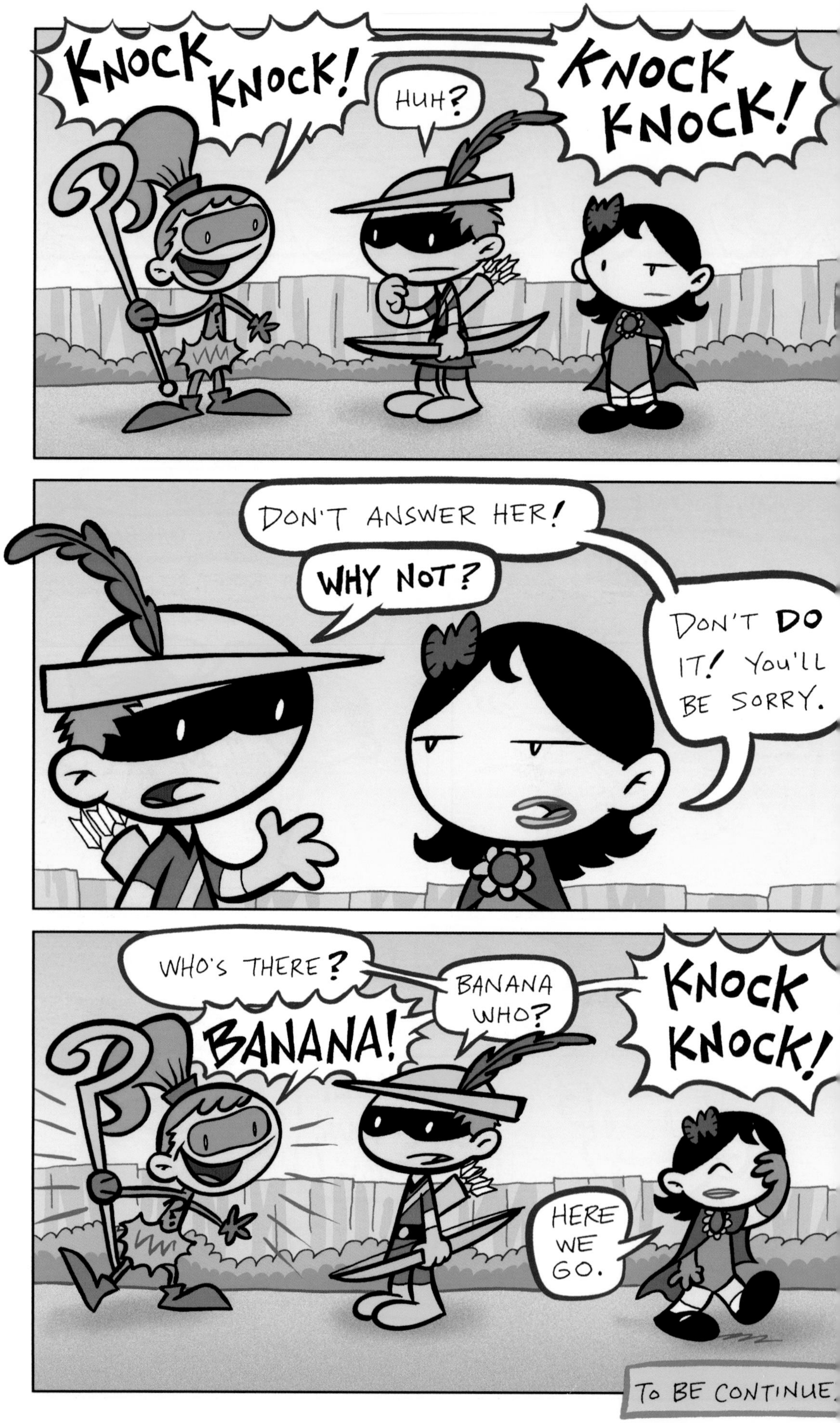
KNOCK KNOCK!
HUH?
KNOCK KNOCK!
DON'T ANSWER HER!
WHY NOT?
DON'T DO IT! YOU'LL BE SORRY.
WHO'S THERE?
BANANA!
BANANA WHO?
KNOCK KNOCK!
HERE WE GO.
TO BE CONTINUE

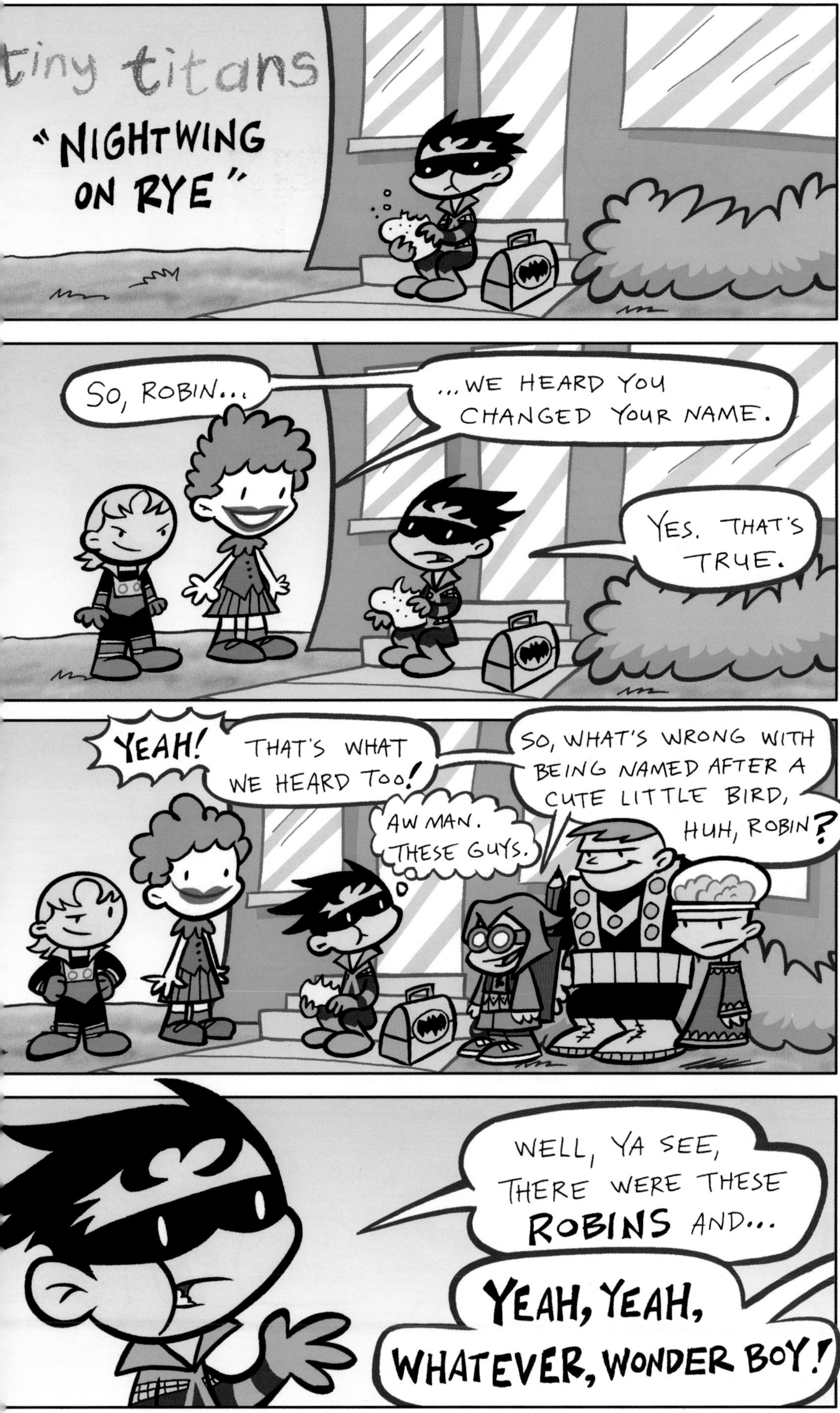
tiny titans
"NIGHTWING ON RYE"
SO, ROBIN...
...WE HEARD YOU CHANGED YOUR NAME.
YES. THAT'S TRUE.
YEAH!
THAT'S WHAT WE HEARD TOO!
SO, WHAT'S WRONG WITH BEING NAMED AFTER A CUTE LITTLE BIRD, HUH, ROBIN?
AW MAN. THESE GUYS.
WELL, YA SEE, THERE WERE THESE ROBINS AND...
YEAH, YEAH, WHATEVER, WONDER BOY!

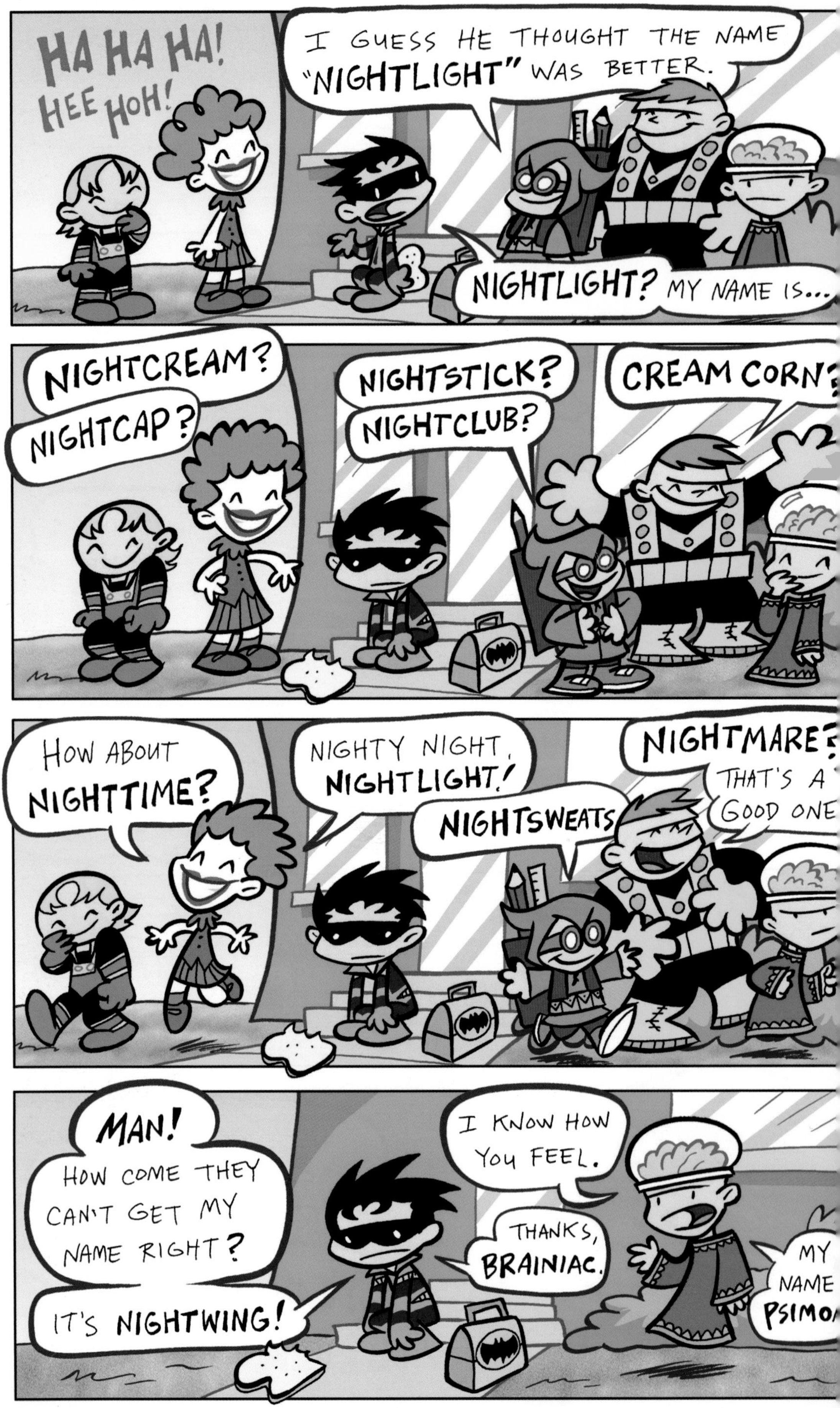
HA HA HA!
HEE HOH!
I GUESS HE THOUGHT THE NAME "NIGHTLIGHT" WAS BETTER.
NIGHTLIGHT? MY NAME IS...
NIGHTCREAM?
NIGHTCAP?
NIGHTSTICK?
NIGHTCLUB?
CREAM CORN
HOW ABOUT NIGHTTIME?
NIGHTY NIGHT, NIGHTLIGHT!
NIGHTSWEATS
NIGHTMARE
THAT'S A GOOD ONE
MAN!
HOW COME THEY CAN'T GET MY NAME RIGHT?
IT'S NIGHTWING!
I KNOW HOW YOU FEEL.
THANKS, BRAINIAC.
MY NAME

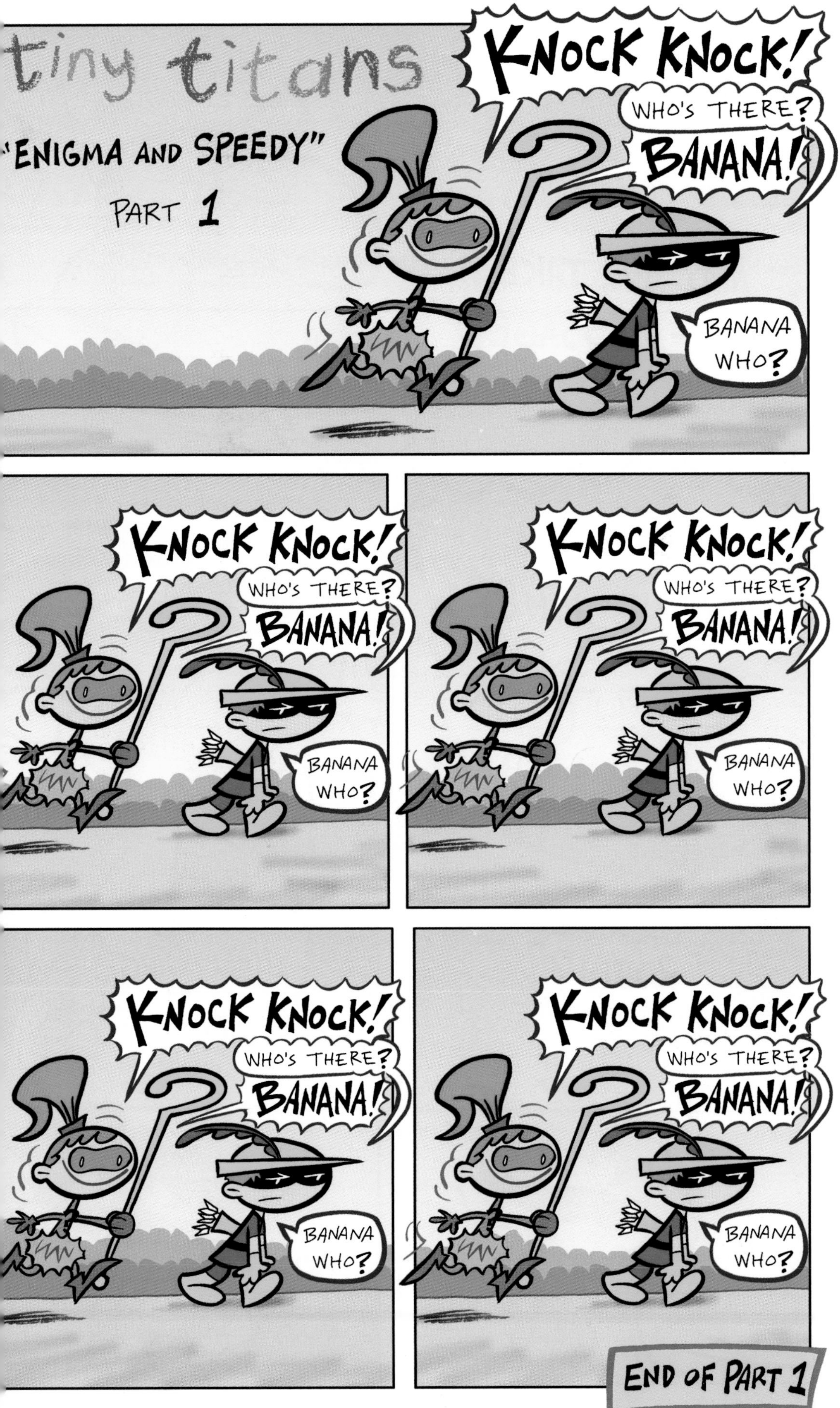
tiny titans
"ENIGMA AND SPEEDY"
PART 1
KNOCK KNOCK!
WHO'S THERE?
BANANA!
BANANA WHO?
KNOCK KNOCK!
WHO'S THERE?
BANANA!
BANANA WHO?
KNOCK KNOCK!
WHO'S THERE?
BANANA!
BANANA WHO?
KNOCK KNOCK!
WHO'S THERE?
BANANA!
BANANA WHO?
KNOCK KNOCK!
WHO'S THERE?
BANANA!
BANANA WHO?
END OF PART 1

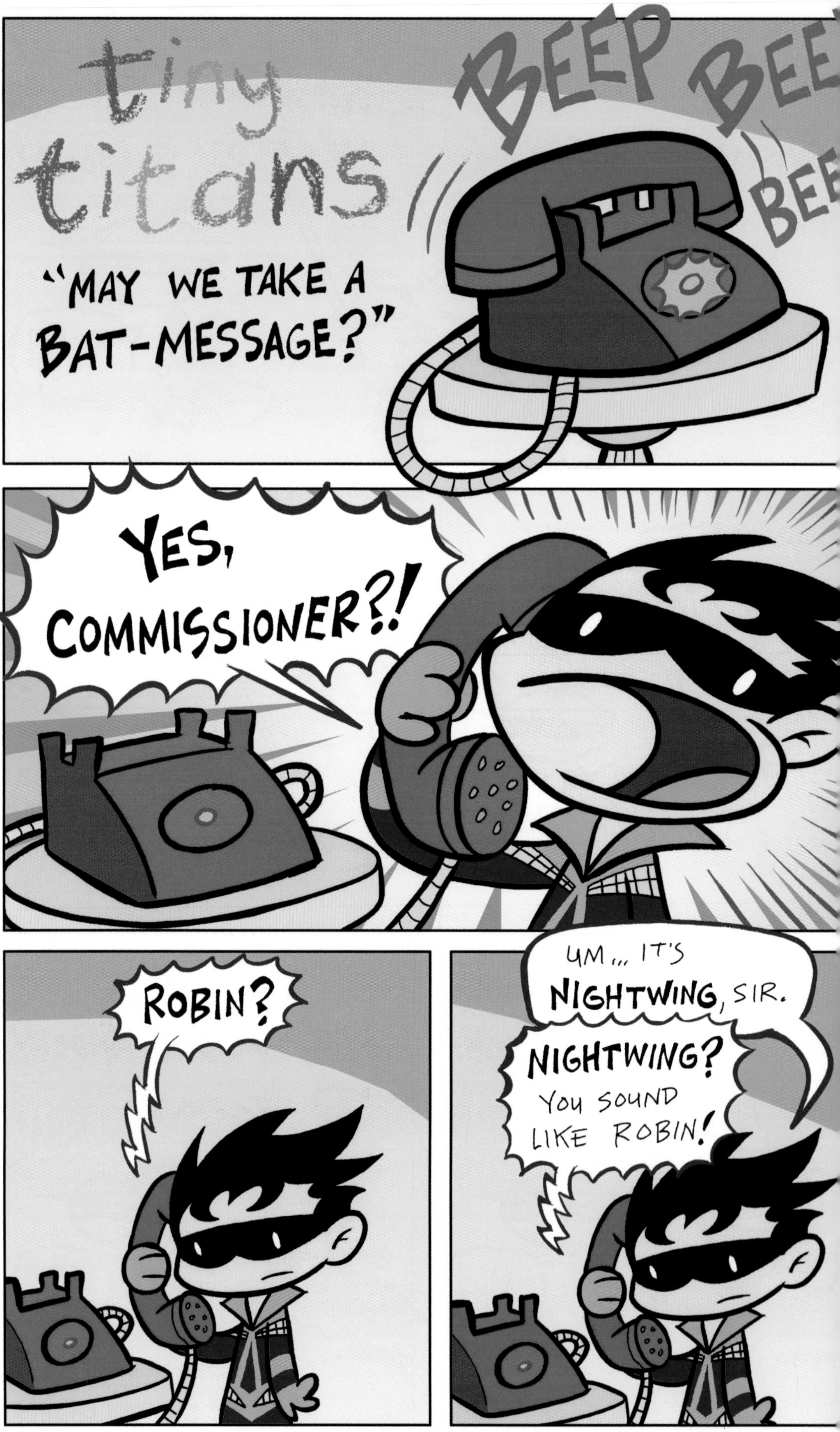
tiny titans
"MAY WE TAKE A BAT-MESSAGE?"
BEEP BEE BEE
YES, COMMISSIONER?!
ROBIN?
UM... IT'S NIGHTWING, SIR.
NIGHTWING? YOU SOUND LIKE ROBIN!

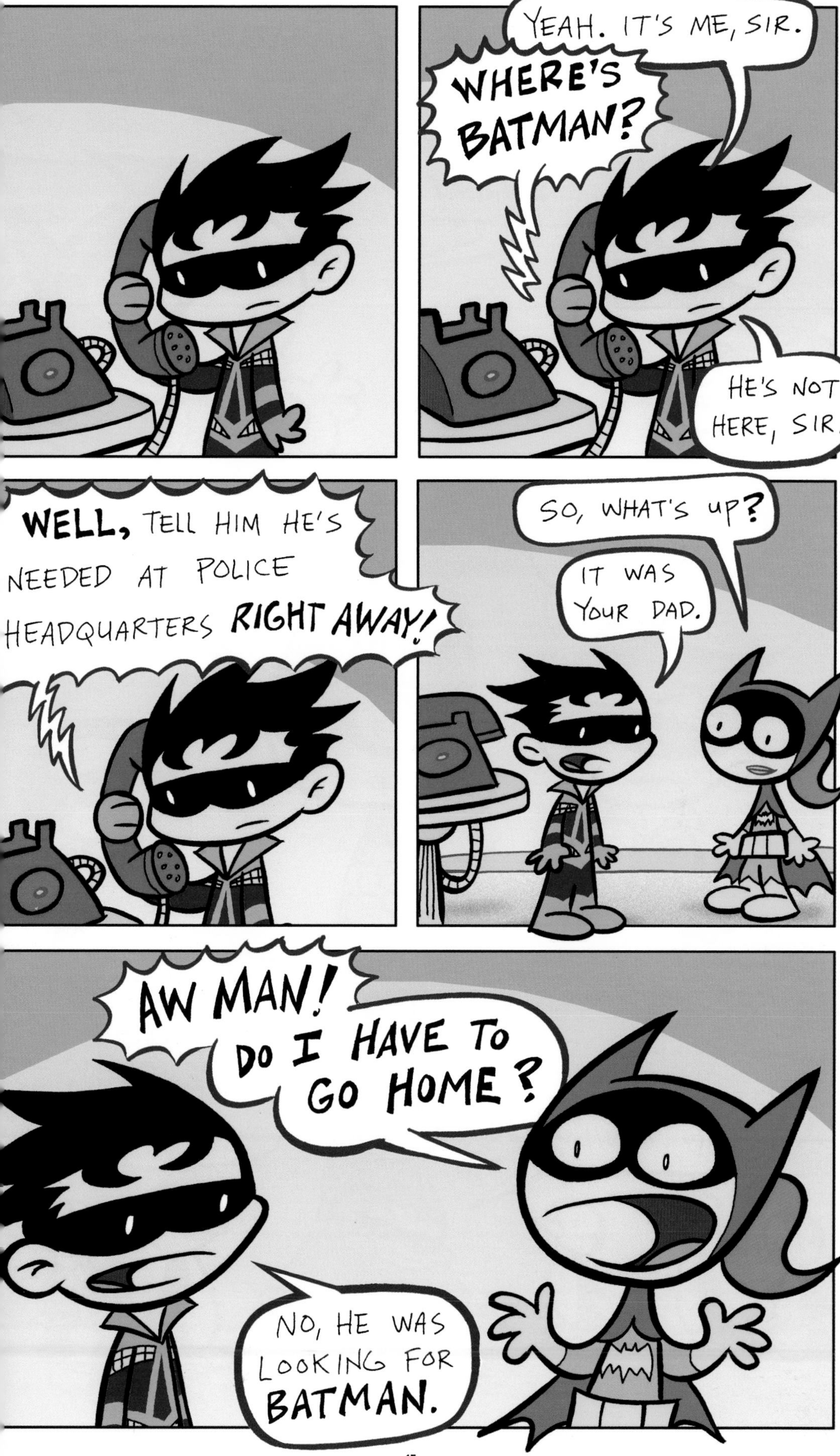
YEAH. IT'S ME, SIR.
WHERE'S BATMAN?
HE'S NOT HERE, SIR.
WELL, TELL HIM HE'S NEEDED AT POLICE HEADQUARTERS RIGHT AWAY!
SO, WHAT'S UP?
IT WAS YOUR DAD.
AW MAN!
DO I HAVE TO GO HOME?
NO, HE WAS LOOKING FOR BATMAN.

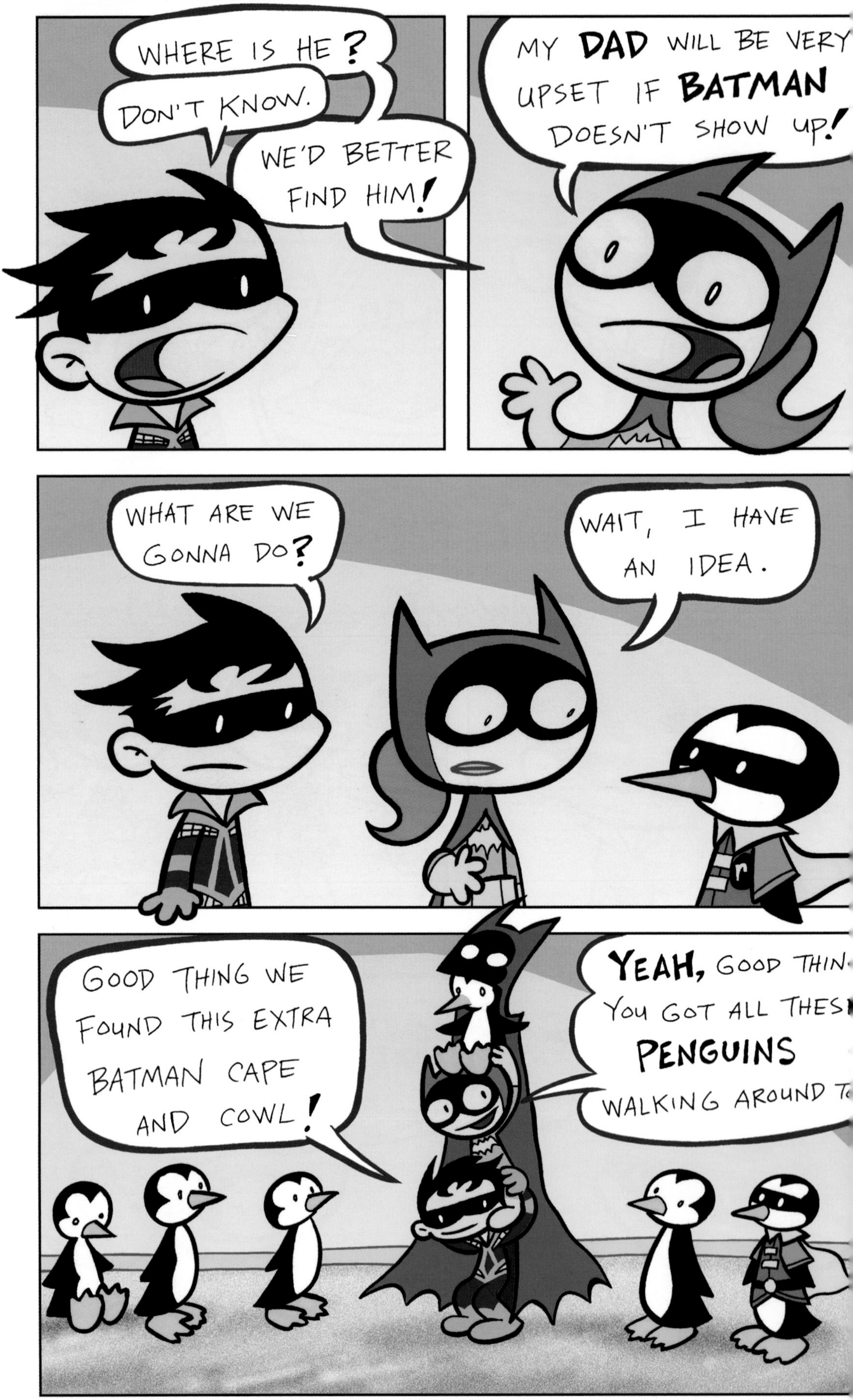
WHERE IS HE?
DON'T KNOW.
WE'D BETTER FIND HIM!
MY **DAD** WILL BE VERY UPSET IF **BATMAN** DOESN'T SHOW UP!
WHAT ARE WE GONNA DO?
WAIT, I HAVE AN IDEA.
GOOD THING WE FOUND THIS EXTRA BATMAN CAPE AND COWL!
YEAH, GOOD THIN
YOU GOT ALL THES
PENGUINS
WALKING AROUND T

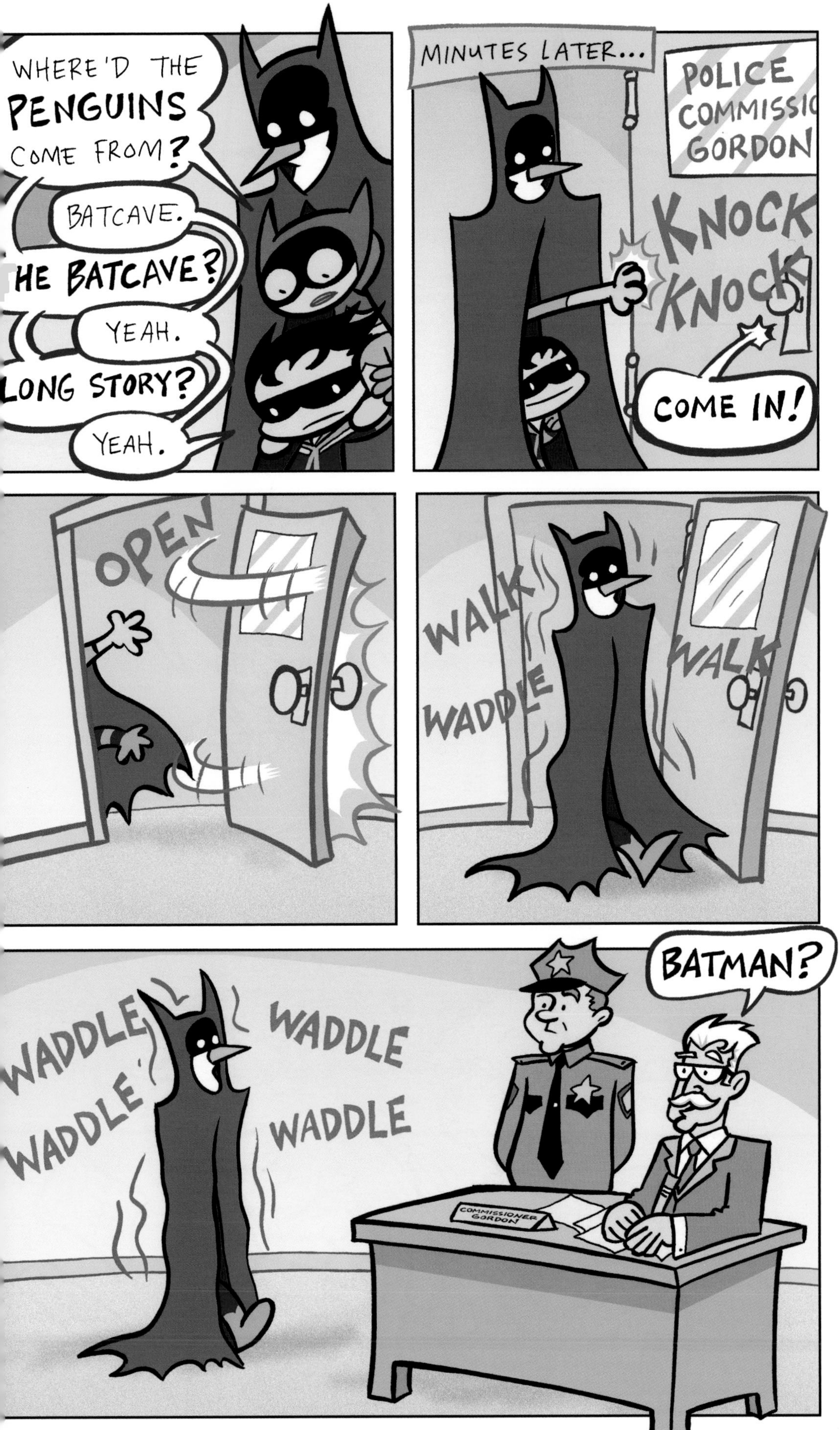
WHERE'D THE PENGUINS COME FROM?
BATCAVE.
HE BATCAVE?
YEAH.
LONG STORY?
YEAH.
MINUTES LATER...
POLICE COMMISSI GORDON
KNOCK KNOCK
COME IN!
OPEN
WALK
WADDLE
WALK
WADDLE
WADDLE
WADDLE
WADDLE
BATMAN?
COMMISSIONER GORDON

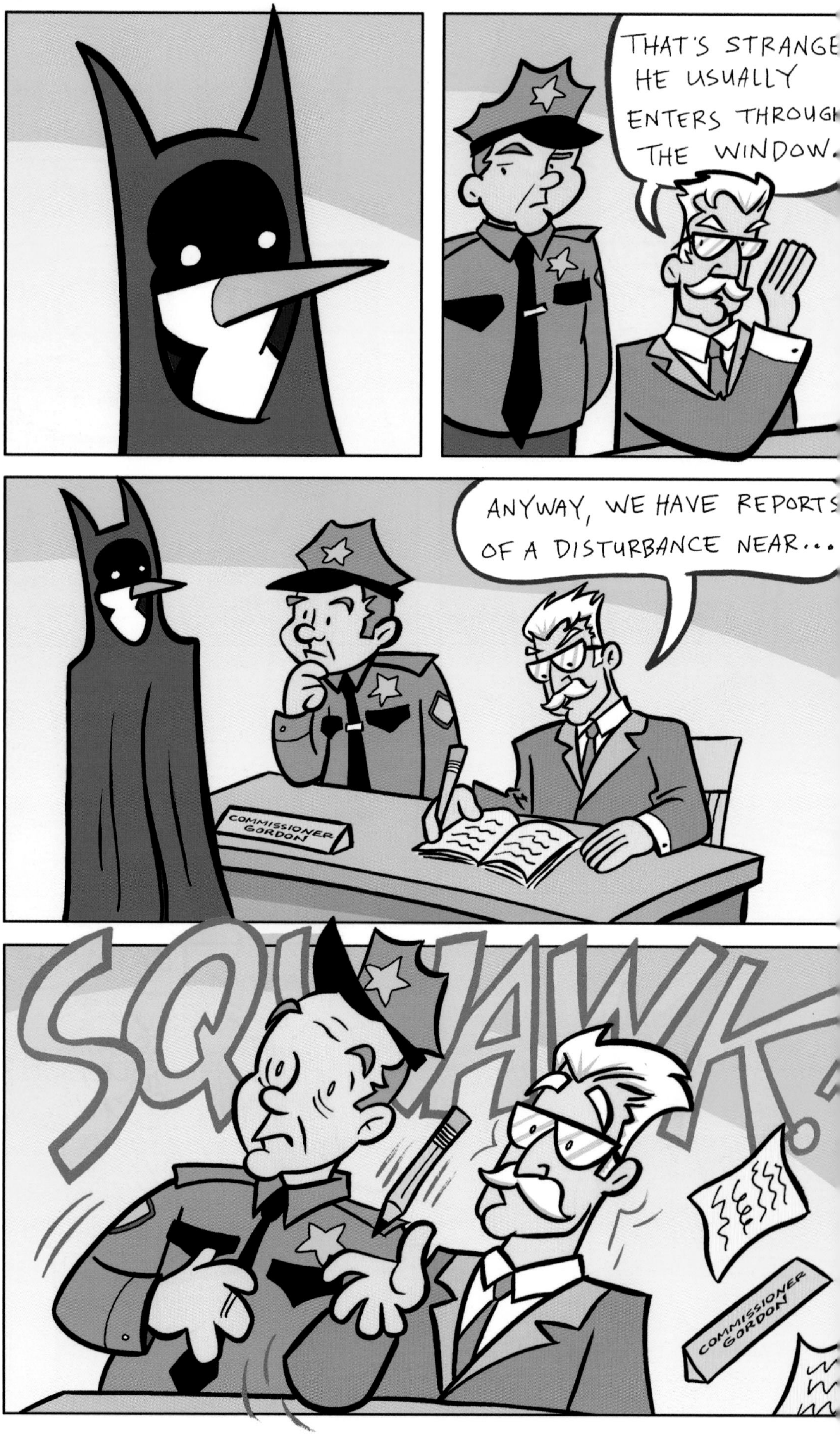
THAT'S STRANGE HE USUALLY ENTERS THROUGH THE WINDOW.
ANYWAY, WE HAVE REPORTS OF A DISTURBANCE NEAR...
COMMISSIONER GORDON
SQUAWK!
COMMISSIONER GORDON

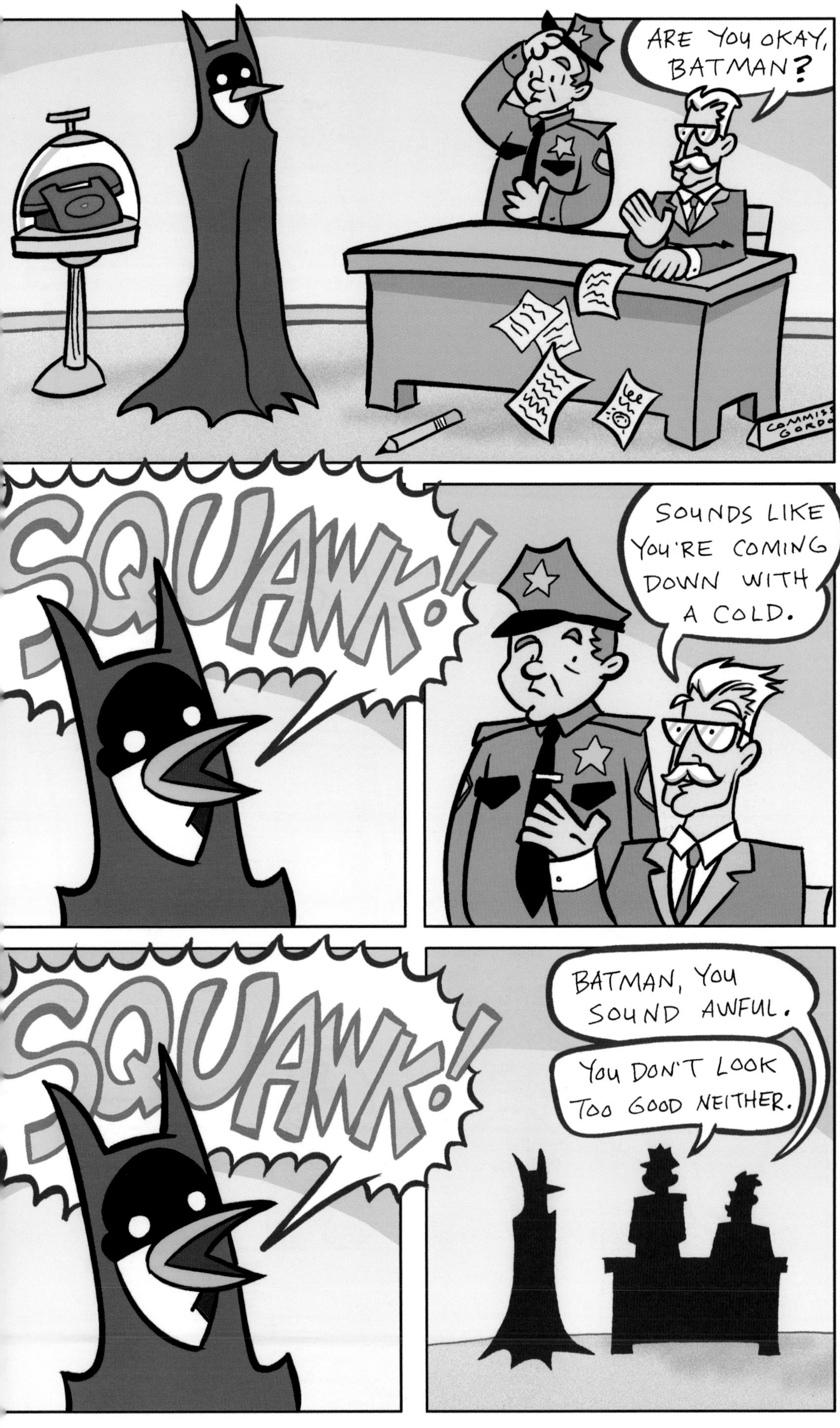
ARE YOU OKAY, BATMAN?
SQUAWK!
SOUNDS LIKE YOU'RE COMING DOWN WITH A COLD.
SQUAWK!
BATMAN, YOU SOUND AWFUL.
YOU DON'T LOOK TOO GOOD NEITHER.

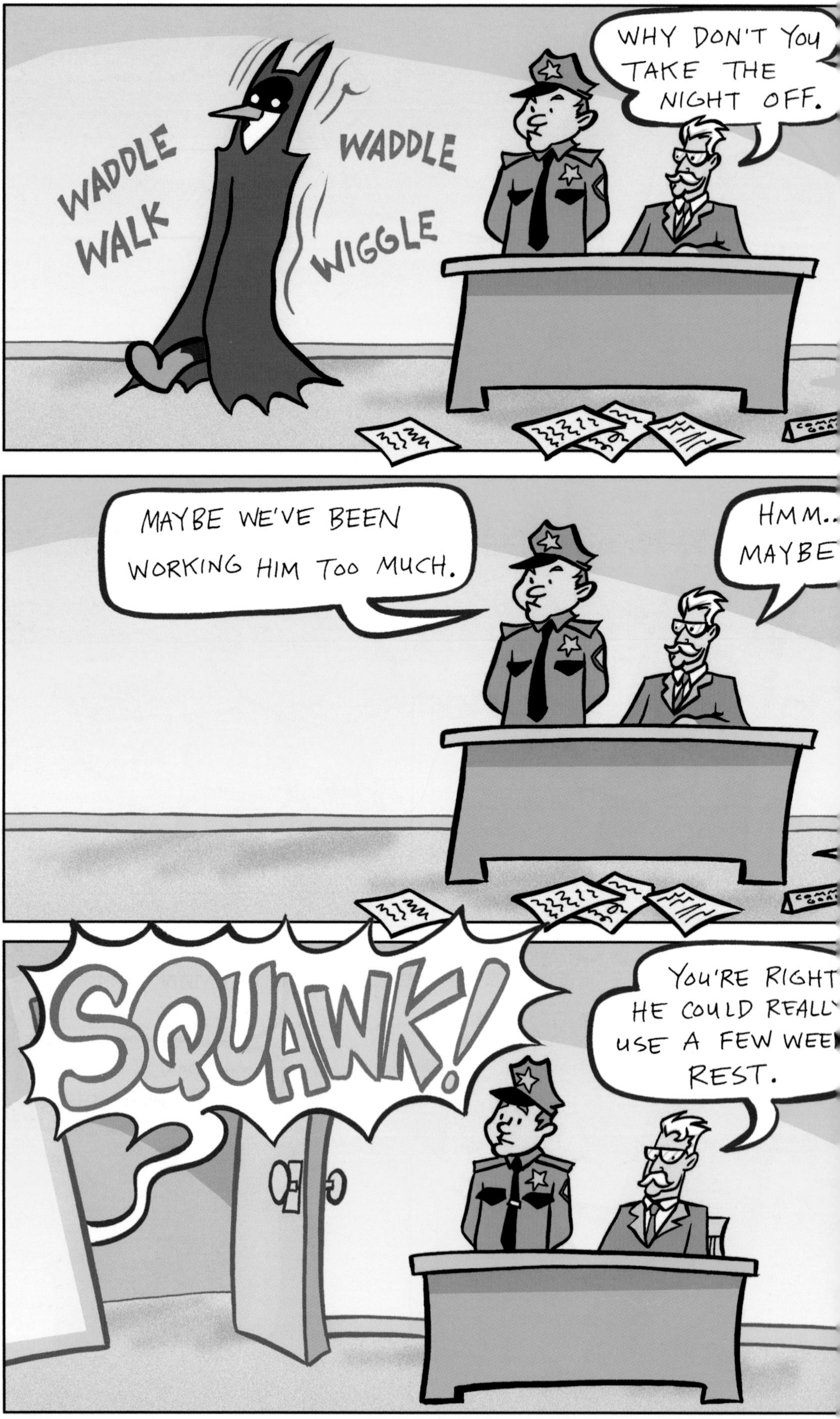
WADDLE
WALK
WADDLE
WIGGLE
WHY DON'T YOU TAKE THE NIGHT OFF.
MAYBE WE'VE BEEN WORKING HIM TOO MUCH.
HMM.. MAYBE
SQUAWK!
YOU'RE RIGHT HE COULD REALL USE A FEW WEE REST.

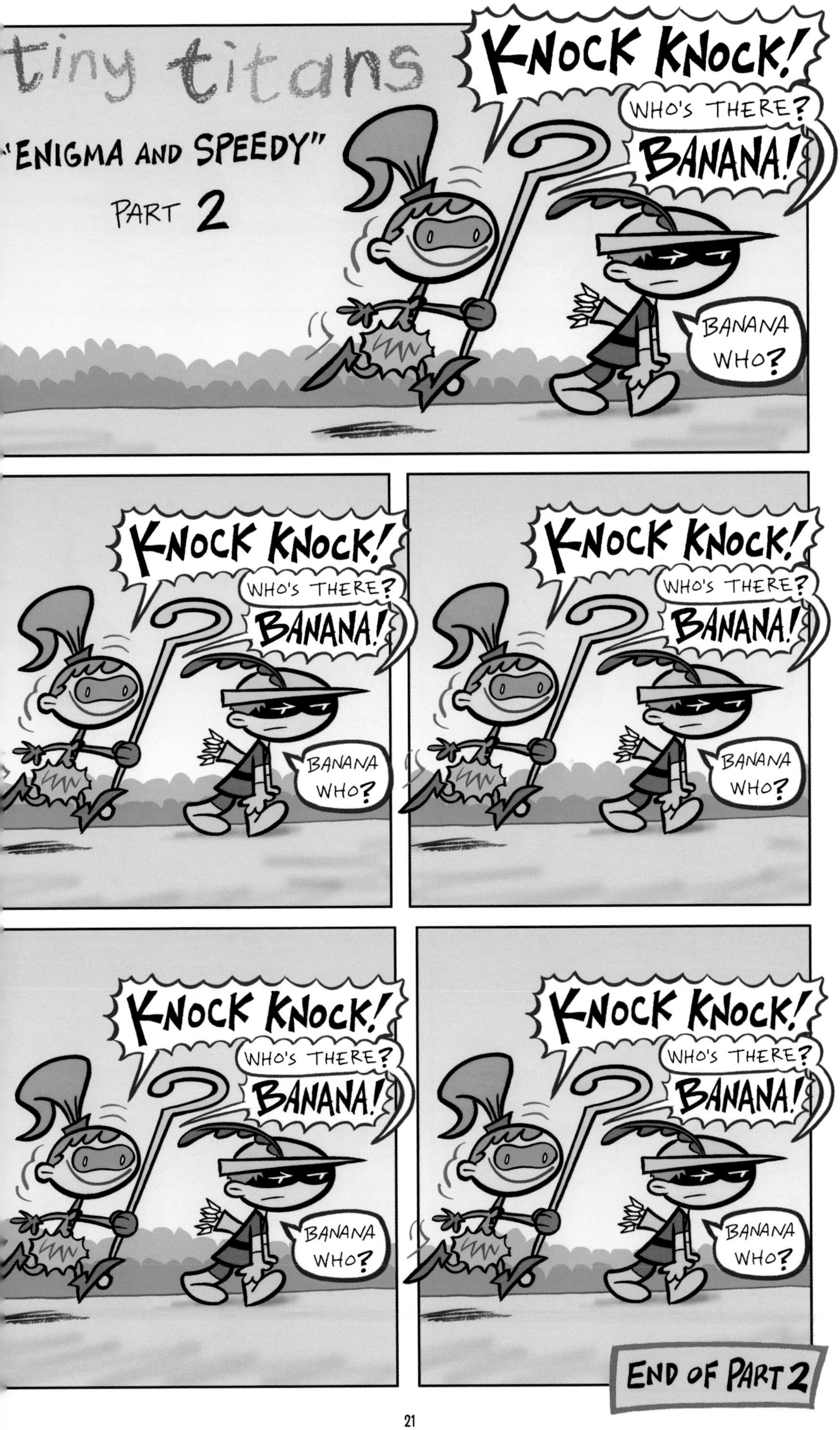
tiny titans
"ENIGMA AND SPEEDY"
PART 2
KNOCK KNOCK!
WHO'S THERE?
BANANA!
BANANA WHO?
KNOCK KNOCK!
WHO'S THERE?
BANANA!
BANANA WHO?
KNOCK KNOCK!
WHO'S THERE?
BANANA!
BANANA WHO?
KNOCK KNOCK!
WHO'S THERE?
BANANA!
BANANA WHO?
KNOCK KNOCK!
WHO'S THERE?
BANANA!
BANANA WHO?
END OF PART 2

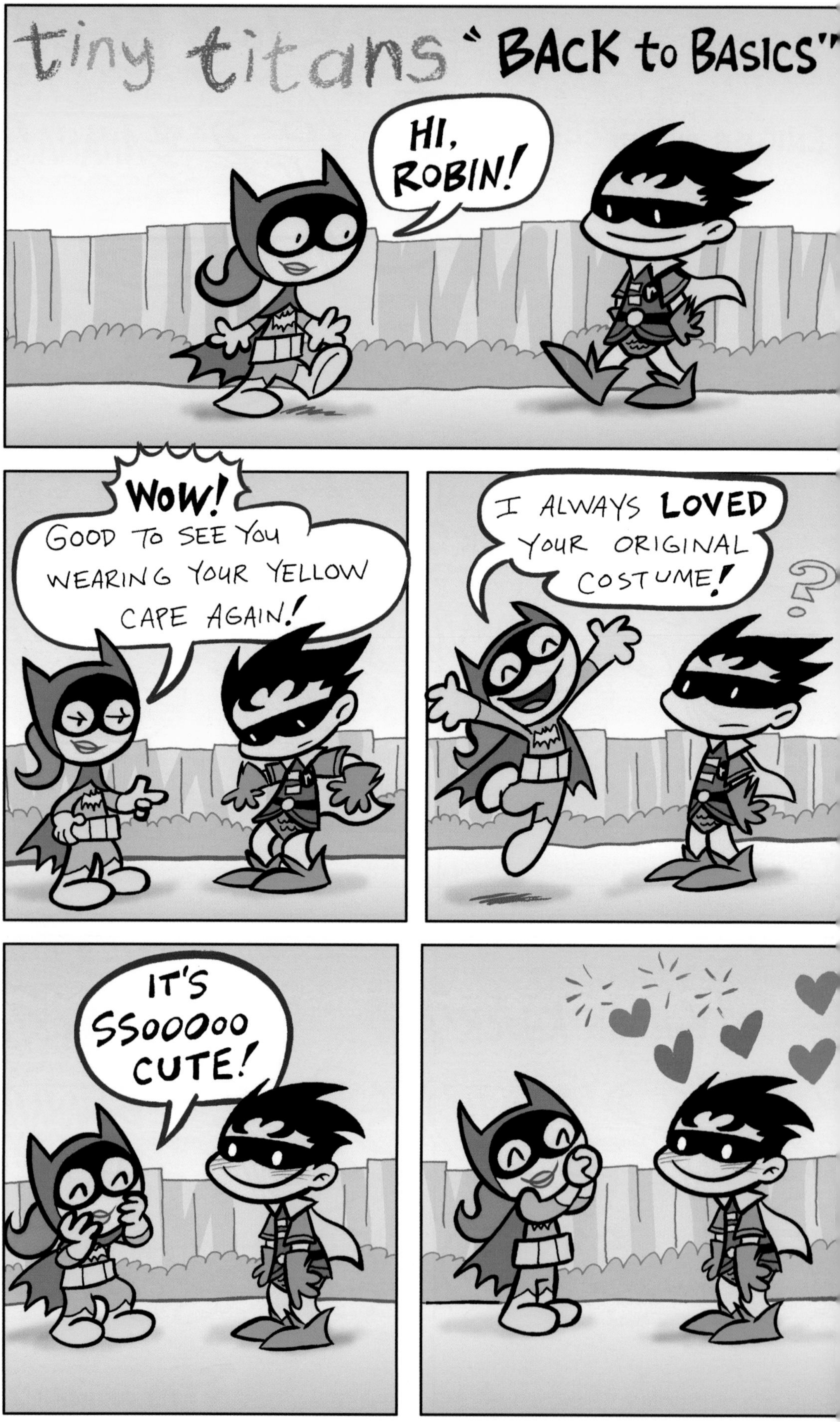
tiny titans "BACK to BASICS"
HI, ROBIN!
WOW! GOOD TO SEE YOU WEARING YOUR YELLOW CAPE AGAIN!
I ALWAYS LOVED YOUR ORIGINAL COSTUME!
?
IT'S SSOOOOO CUTE!

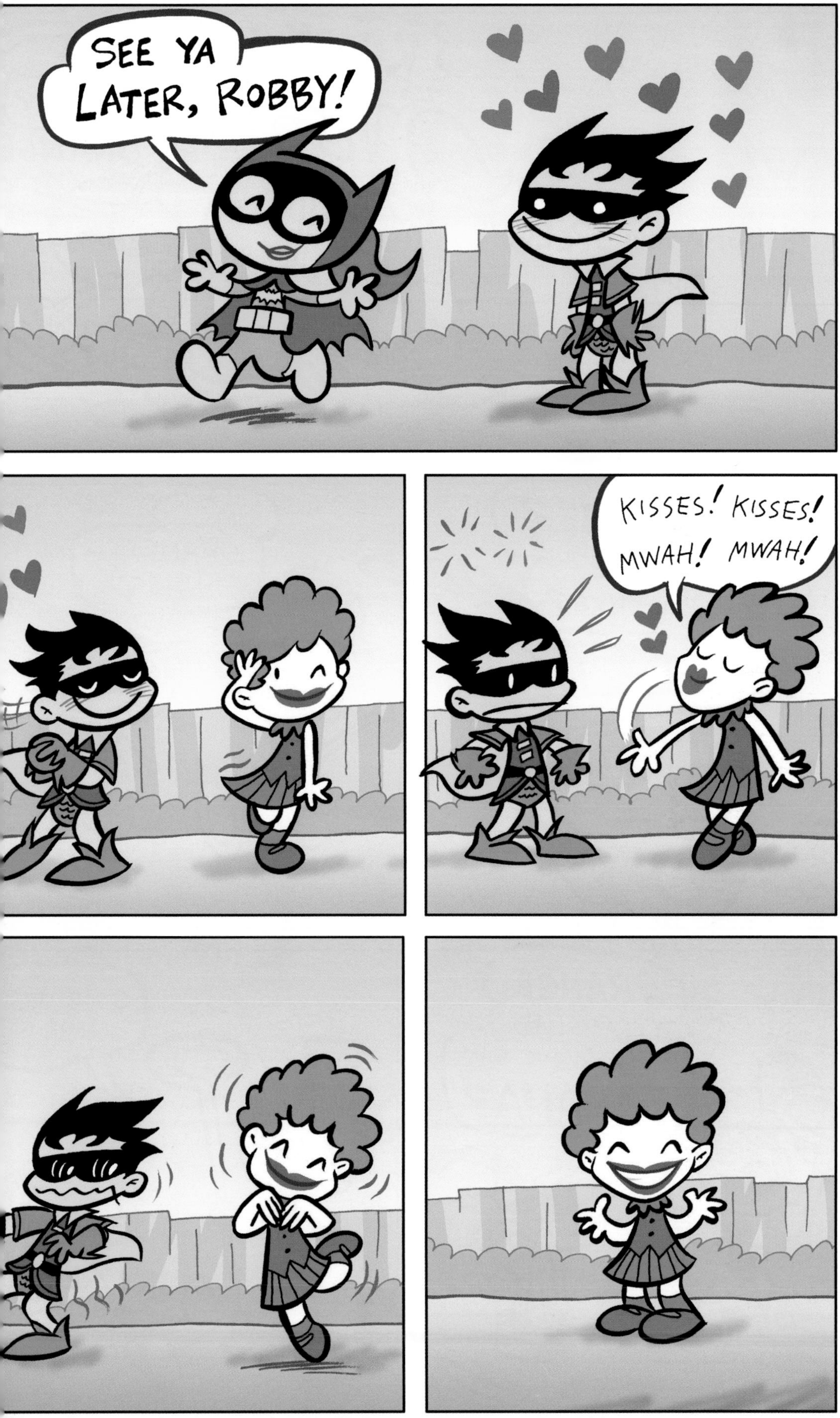
SEE YA LATER, ROBBY!
KISSES! KISSES! MWAH! MWAH!

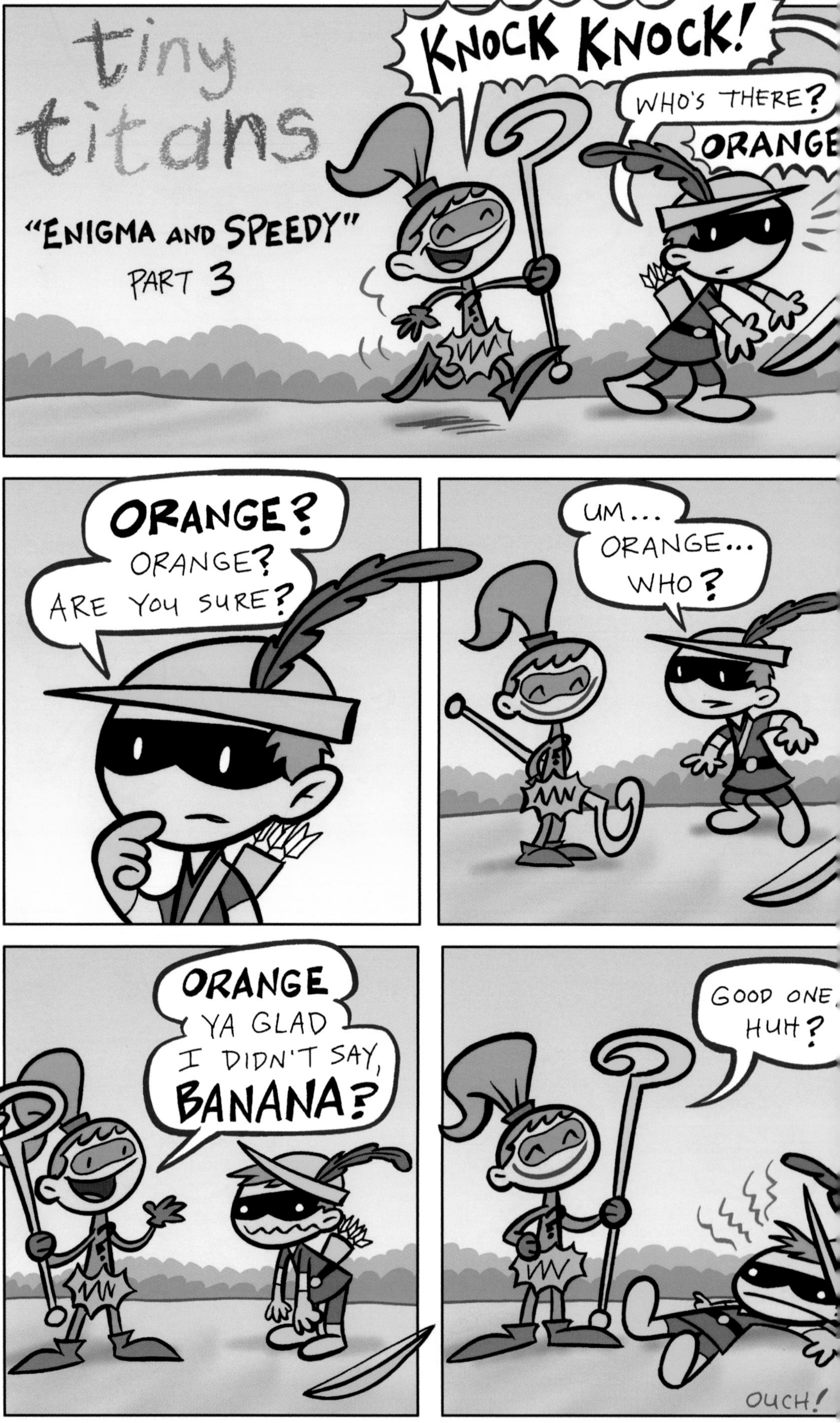
tiny titans
"ENIGMA AND SPEEDY"
PART 3
KNOCK KNOCK!
WHO'S THERE?
ORANGE
ORANGE? ORANGE? ARE YOU SURE?
UM... ORANGE... WHO?
ORANGE YA GLAD I DIDN'T SAY, BANANA?
GOOD ONE, HUH?
OUCH!

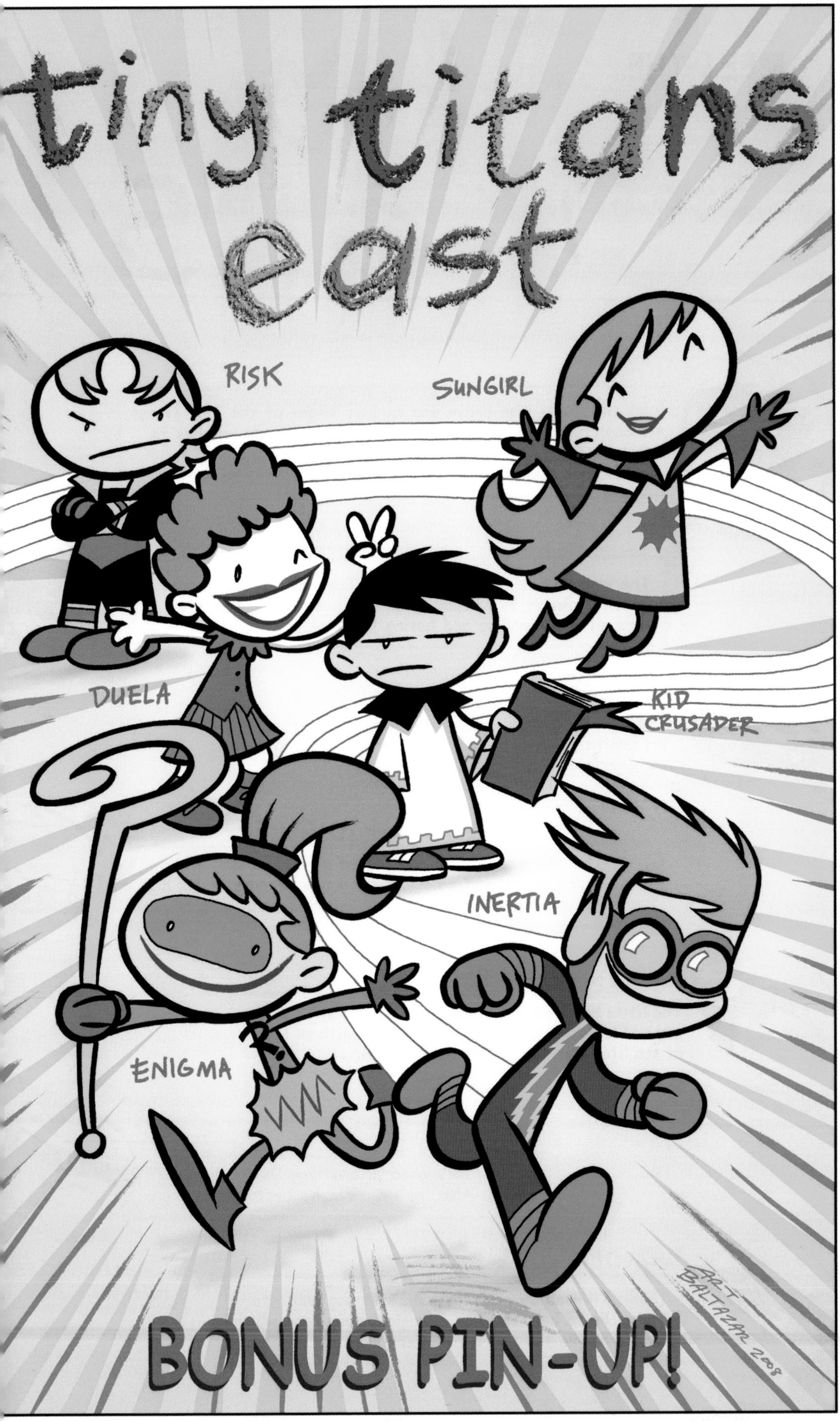
tiny titans east
RISK
SUNGIRL
DUELA
KID CRUSADER
INERTIA
ENIGMA
ART BALTAZAR 2008
BONUS PIN-UP!

MEET THE... *tiny titans*

ROBIN

(Dick Grayson)- The brave and serious leader of the Tiny Titans. Although he is the original Robin, he is very moody and has to share his room with his brothers, the other Robins. Also, he has secret crushes for Starfire and Barbara Gordon.

JASON TODDLER

The youngest of the three Robins. Too young to go to school, Jason is always in a happy mood and has a care-free style. He's all about smiling and having fun.

TIM DRAKE

The cool Robin. Tim wants to stand out from his brothers by wearing his own unique Robin costume. He's very laid back and easy going indeed.

KID FLASH

The super speedster and fasted kid in the school. Quick witted and eats lots for lunch because of his high metabolism. Too much candy will cause major sugar rush.

AQUALAD

The little boy from the ocean. Has a pet fish named Fluffy. Aqualad can communicate with all forms of sea life, even the pet hamster in their classroom.

SPEEDY

Quiet and cool, he is the boy with the trick arrows. He's good at anything that requires aiming. Also, he's Kid Flash's best friend.

WONDER GIRL

(Donna) Raised by amazons. She's strong and cute. Never lie to her, she has a magical jump rope which makes people tell the truth. Very skeptic.

RAVEN

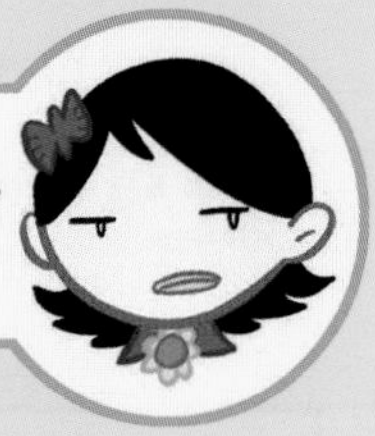

The quiet and mysterious little girl. She really likes to experiment with dark magic, which usually turn into bad practical jokes. Mr. Trigon, the substitute teacher is her father.

CYBORG

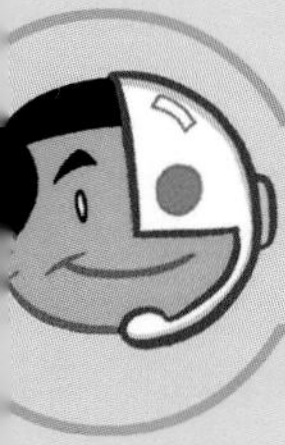

Half boy, half robot. Cyborg is always tinkering with mechanical gadgets, often turning them into something else. His battle cry "BOO-YA!" has earned him the nickname, "Big Boo-Ya".

BEAST BOY

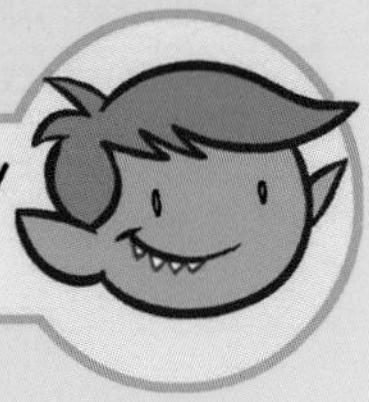

The green little boy who can change into any animal he desires. He's a prankster and loves comics. Has a crush on Terra.

STARFIRE

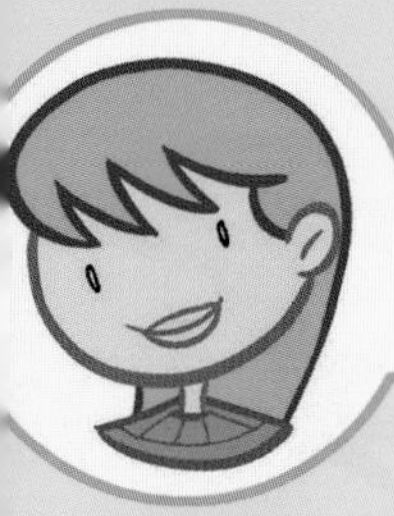

She's an alien princess. Very naïve and free spirited and finds the good in others. Has a crush on Robin and thinks he's cute, but so do all the other girls.

KID DEVIL

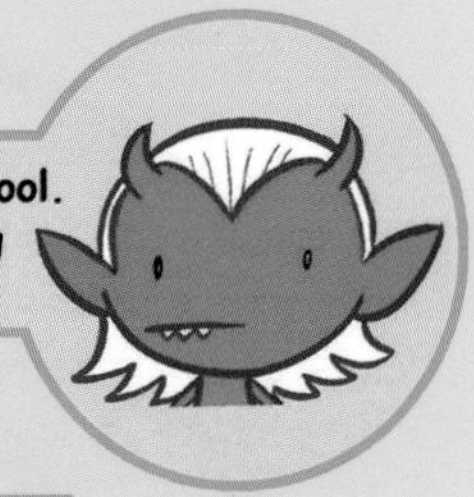

One of the younger Tiny Titans, still too young for school. Cannot talk but can breathe fire, usually while coughing or sneezing or hiccupping.

ROSE & JERICHO

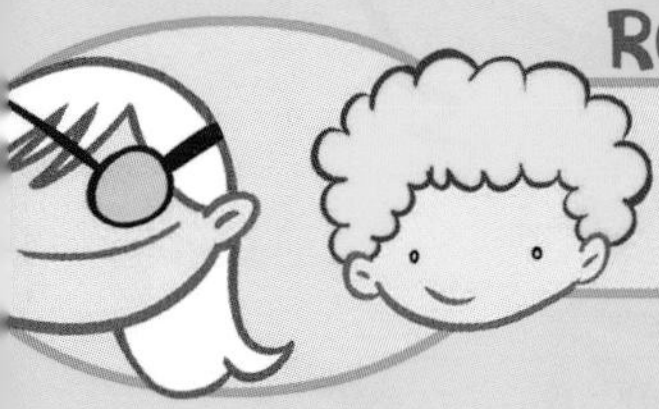

Principal Slade's kids. Rose is the older and tougher "Tom-Boy" of the two. Jericho can't speak, but can take over your mind if you look into his eyes.

MISS MARTIAN

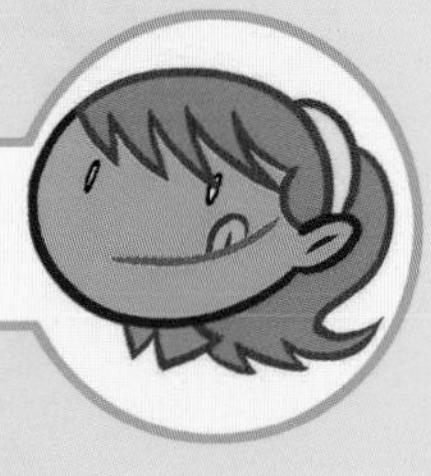

A shape shifting little girl alien from Mars who is still too young to go to school. She is often mistaken for Beast Boy's little sister.

TERRA

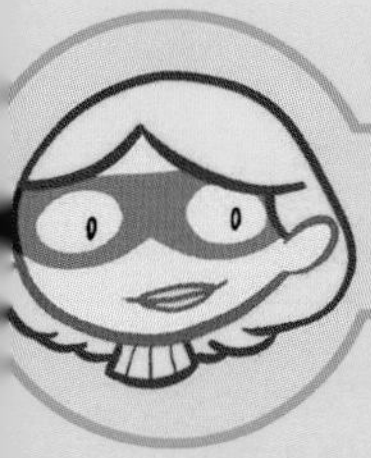

The sometimes hated little girl who likes to throw rocks. Principal Slade's teacher's pet. She thinks Beast Boy is a weirdo.

CASSIE

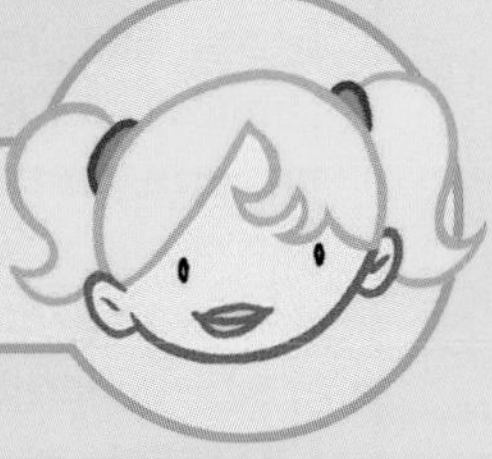

Wonder Girl's rich cousin from the big city. Cassie's really into fashion and is hip to all the latest trends in POP culture.

BUMBLE BEE

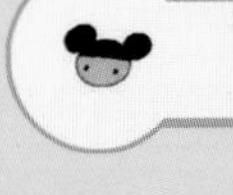

The tiniest of the Tiny Titans.
BB buzzes and packs a mighty stinger.

Creators

Art Baltazar is a cartoonist machine from the heart of Chicago! He defines cartoons and comics not only as an art style, but as a way of life. Currently, Art is the creative force behind *The New York Times* best-selling, Eisner Award-winning, DC Comics series Tiny Titans, and the co-writer for Billy Batson and the Magic of SHAZAM! and co-creator of Superman Family Adventures. Art is living the dream! He draws comics and never has to leave the house. He lives with his lovely wife, Rose, big boy Sonny, little boy Gordon, and little girl Audrey. Right on!

ART BALTAZAR

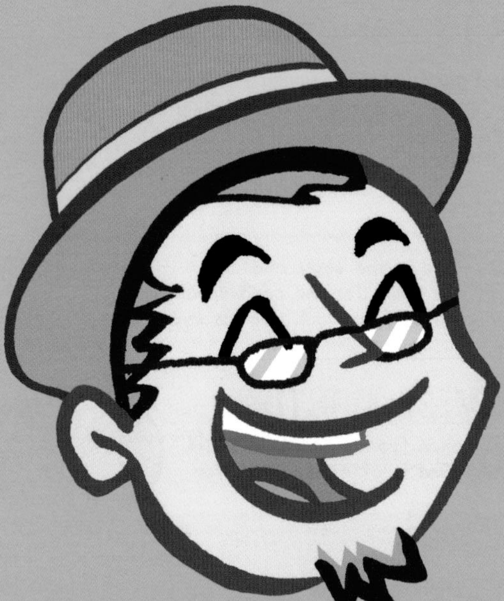

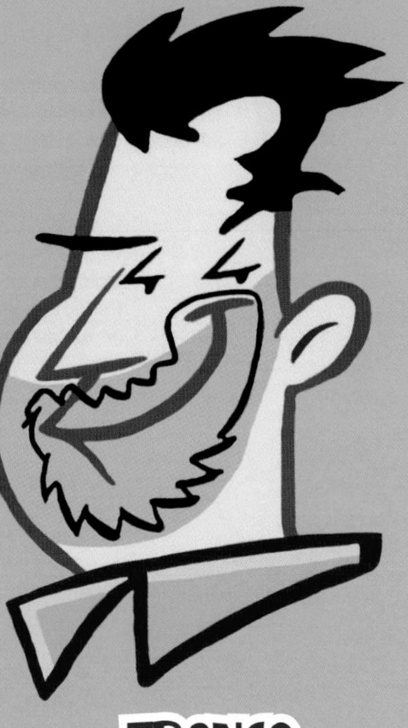

FRANCO

Bronx, New York born writer and artist Franco Aureliani has been drawing comics since he could hold a crayon. Currently residing in upstate New York with his wife, Ivette, and son, Nicolas, Franco spends most of his days in a Batcave-like studio where he produces DC's Tiny Titans comics. In 1995, Franco founded Blindwolf Studios, an independent art studio where he and fellow creators can create children's comics. Franco is the creator, artist, and writer of Weirdsville, L'il Creeps, and Eagle All Star, as well as the co-creator and writer of Patrick the Wolf Boy. When he's not writing and drawing, Franco also teaches high school art.

Glossary

COMMISSIONER [kuh-MISH-uh-nur] - an official in charge of a government department, such as the police

COSTUME [KOSS-toom] - clothes worn by people dressing in disguise

COWL [KOU-uhl] - a long hooded cloak

DISTURBANCE [diss-TUR-benss] - a public commotion or disorder

HEADQUARTERS [HED-kwor-turz] - the place from which an organization is run

RYE [RYE] - a dark brown bread made from rye flour

SIGNAL [SIG-nuhl] - anything agreed upon to send a message or warning, as in the Bat Signal

Joke Time

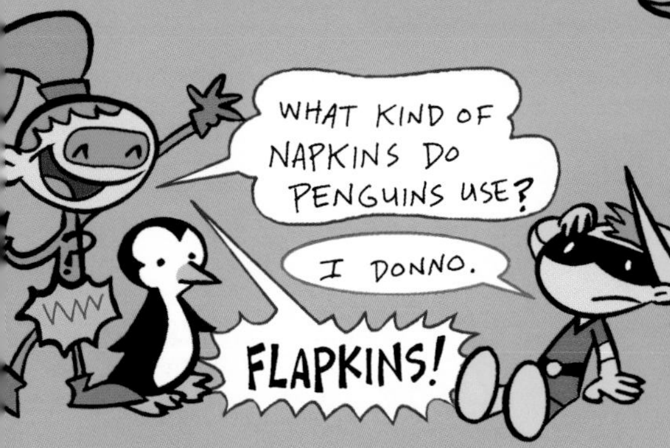
WHAT KIND OF NAPKINS DO PENGUINS USE?
I DONNO.
FLAPKINS!

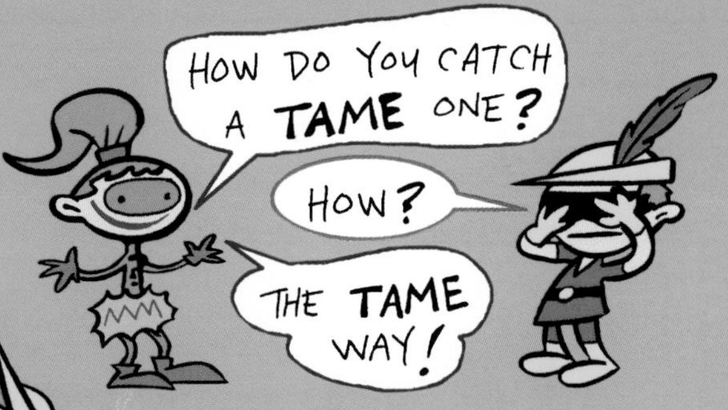
HOW DO YOU CATCH A TAME ONE?
HOW?
THE TAME WAY!

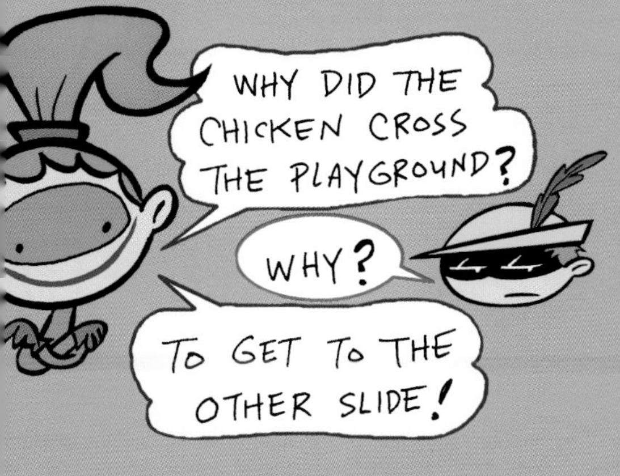
WHY DID THE CHICKEN CROSS THE PLAYGROUND?
WHY?
TO GET TO THE OTHER SLIDE!

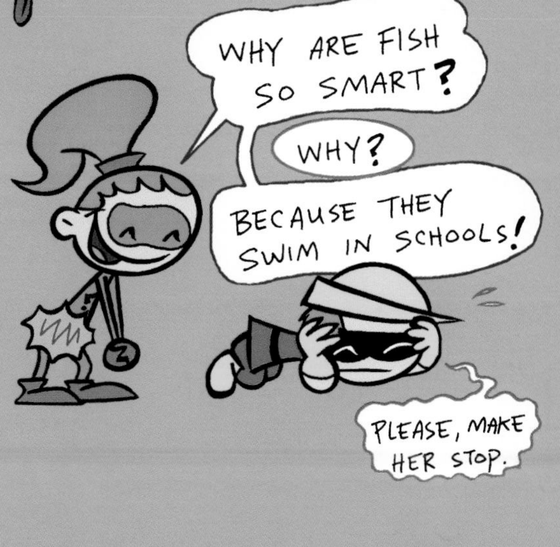
WHY ARE FISH SO SMART?
WHY?
BECAUSE THEY SWIM IN SCHOOLS!
PLEASE, MAKE HER STOP.

Visual Questions & Prompts

1. THE TWO PANELS BELOW APPEAR ALMOST IDENTICAL, BUT SOMETHING HAS CHANGED. HOW CAN YOU TELL WHAT ACTION HAS HAPPENED IN BETWEEN?

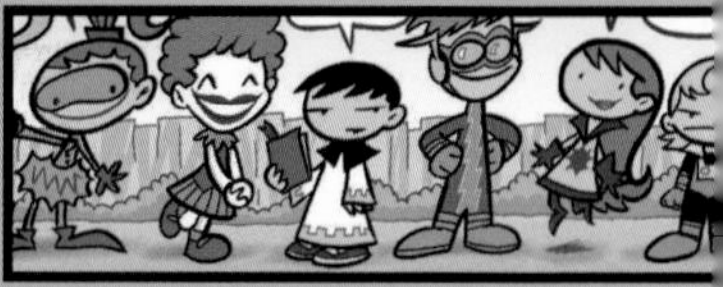

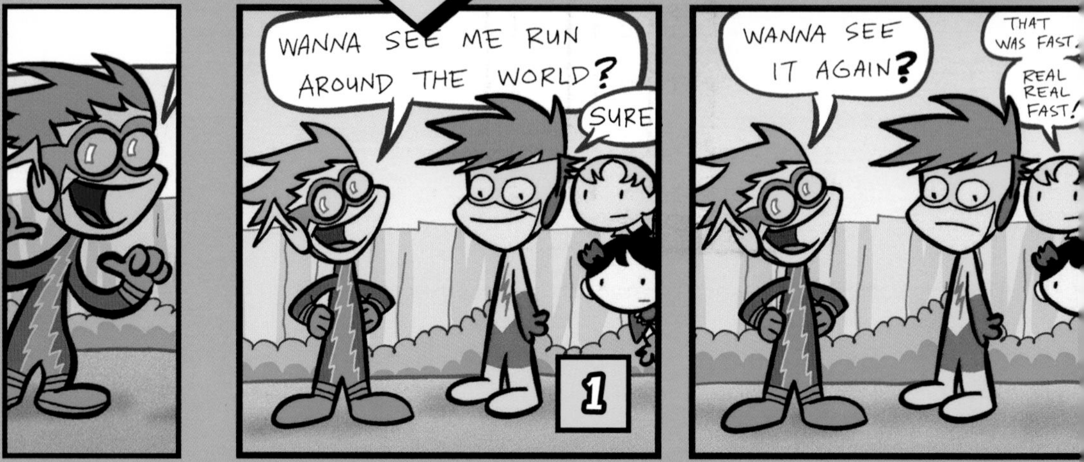
WANNA SEE ME RUN AROUND THE WORLD?
SURE
1
WANNA SEE IT AGAIN?
THAT WAS FAST.
REAL REAL FAST!

2. HOW DO YOU THINK THE TINY TITANS FEEL ABOUT MEETING THE TITANS FROM THE EAST SIDE OF THE PLAYGROUND? WHAT CAN YOU TELL FROM THE LOOKS ON THEIR FACES?

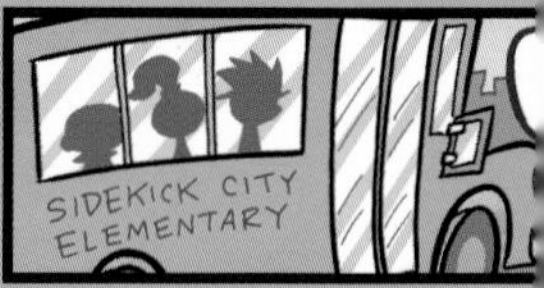
SIDEKICK CITY ELEMENTARY

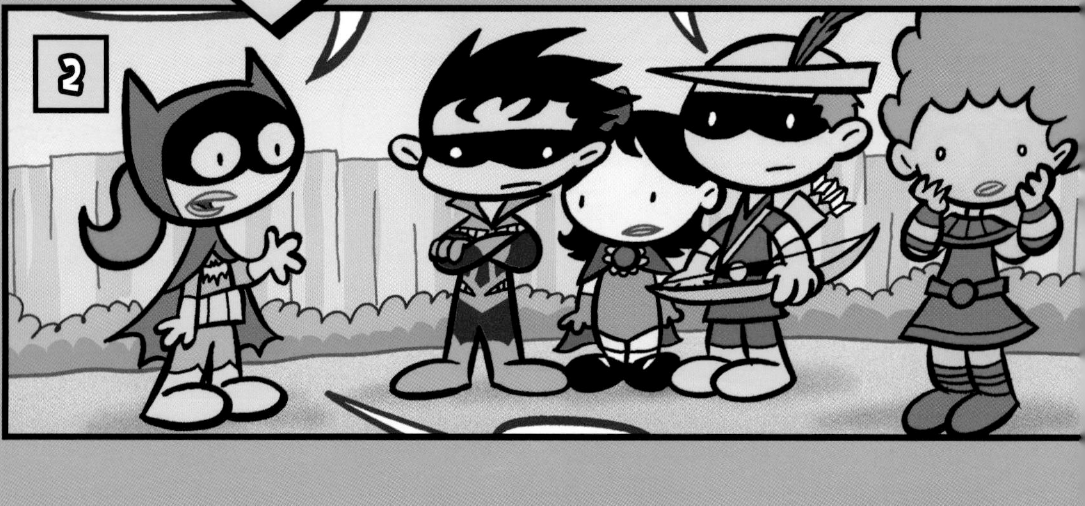
2

3. HOW CAN YOU TELL WHAT ROBIN IS FEELING WHEN THE OTHER TITANS GIVE HIM A HARD TIME ABOUT CHANGING HIS NAME?

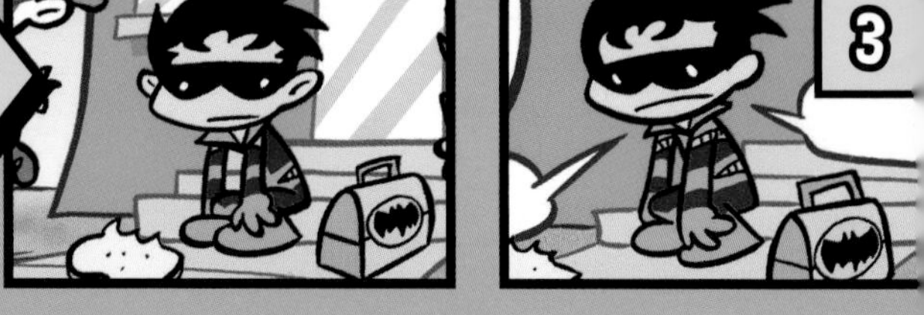
3

4. BASED ON WHAT YOU SEE IN THE PANEL AT RIGHT, EXPLAIN WHAT BATGIRL'S IDEA IS.

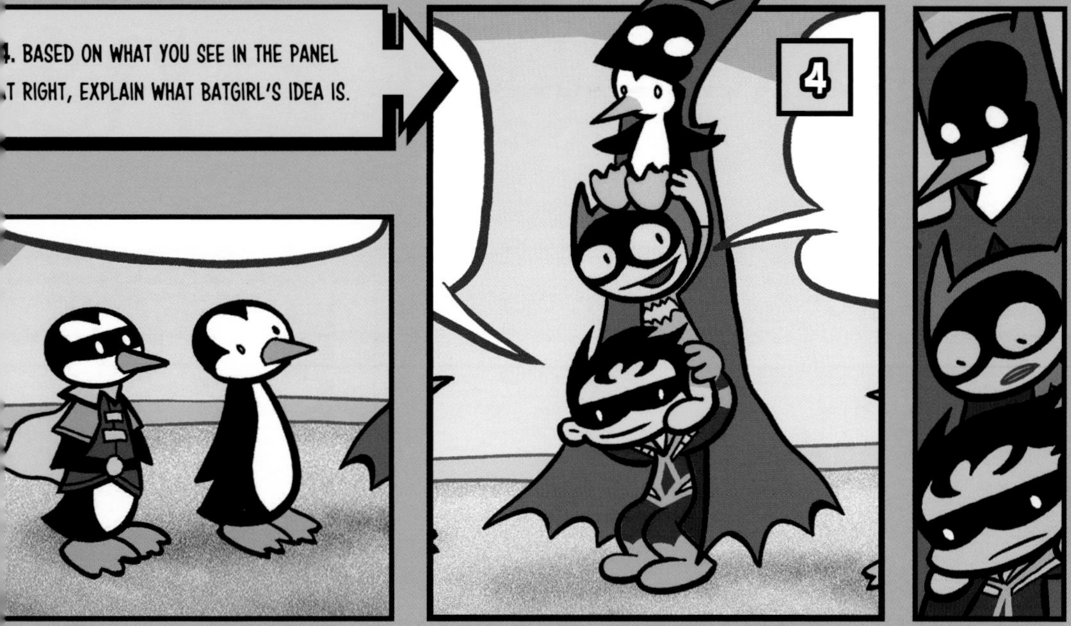
4

5. IMAGINE WHAT IS HAPPENING AFTER "BATMAN" LEAVES THE OFFICE. WRITE 2-3 SENTENCES DESCRIBING THE ACTION YOU DON'T SEE.

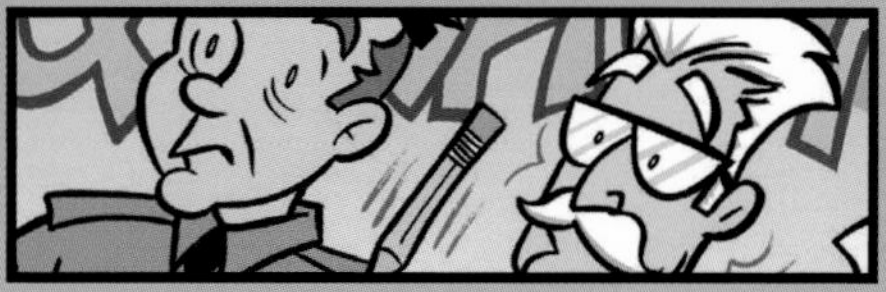

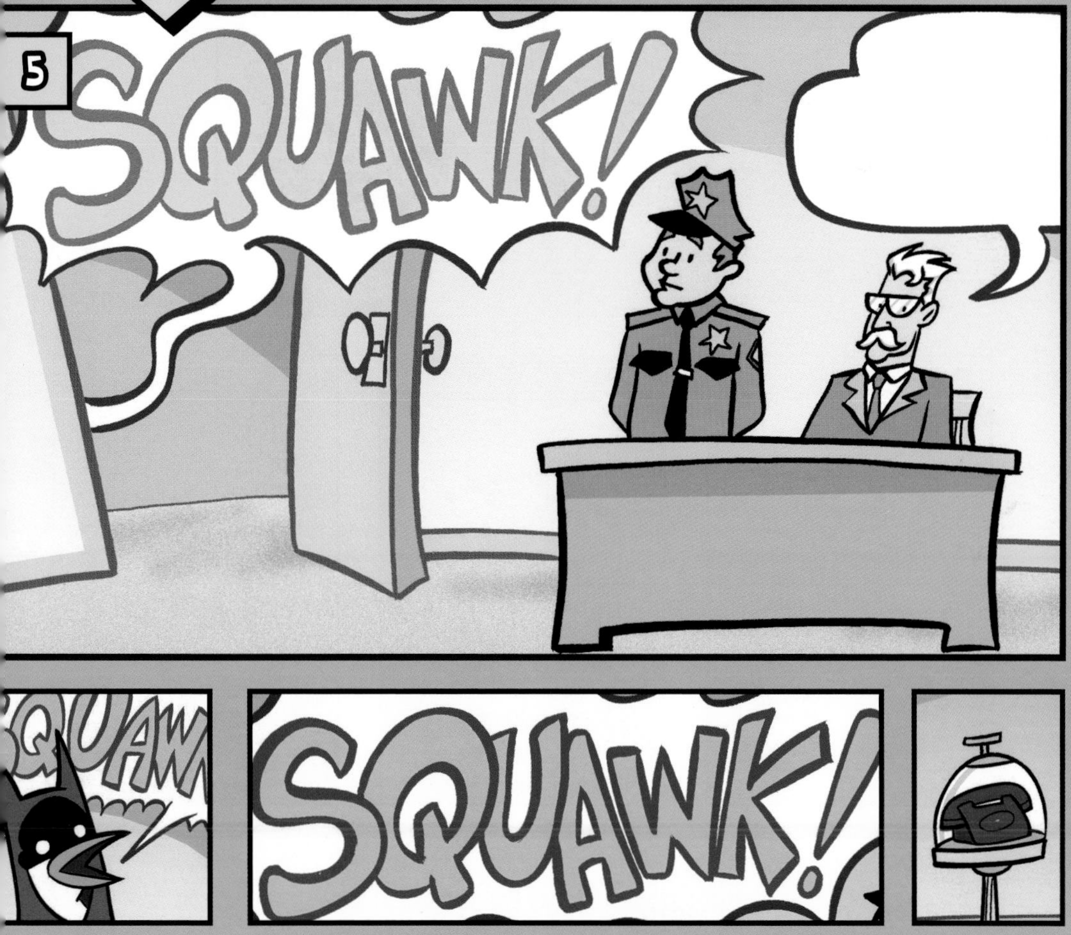
5
SQUAWK!
SQUAW
SQUAWK!

tiny titans

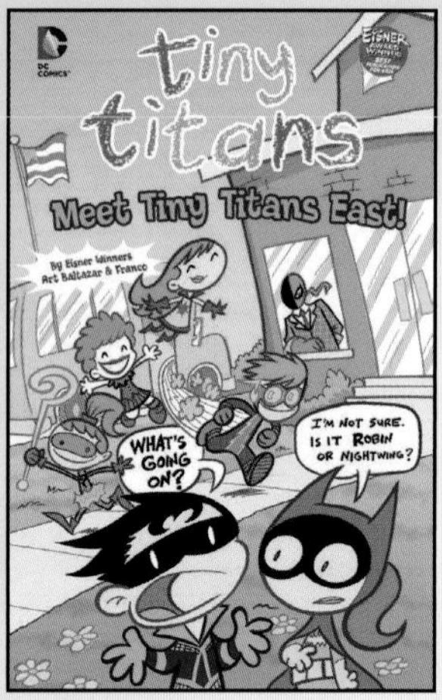
tiny titans
Meet Tiny Titans East!
By Eisner Winners Art Baltazar & Franco
WHAT'S GOING ON?
I'M NOT SURE. IS IT ROBIN OR NIGHTWING?

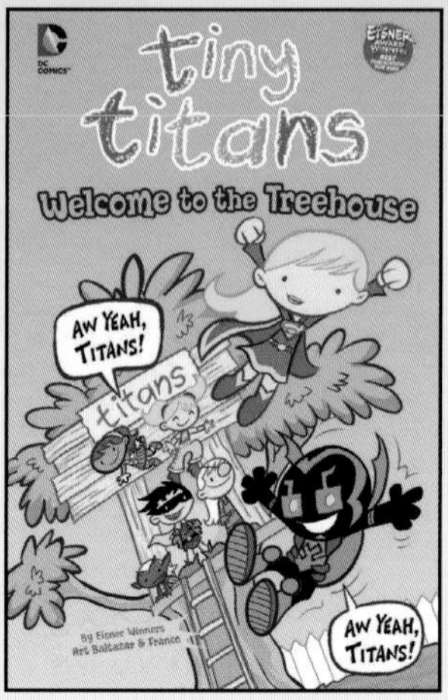
tiny titans
Welcome to the Treehouse
AW YEAH, TITANS!
titans
AW YEAH, TITANS!
By Eisner Winners Art Baltazar & Franco

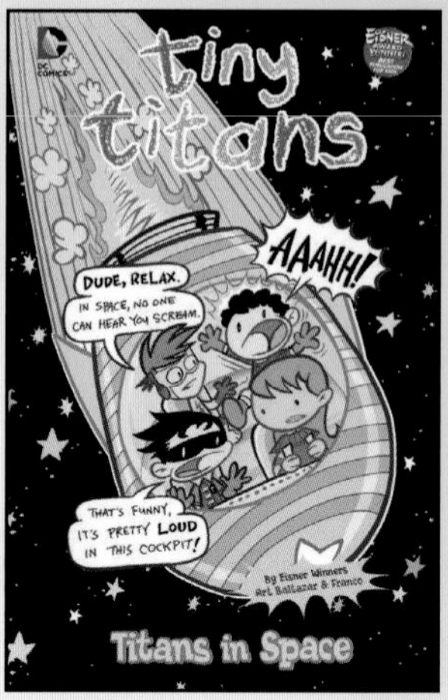
tiny titans
DUDE, RELAX. IN SPACE, NO ONE CAN HEAR YOU SCREAM.
AAAHH!
THAT'S FUNNY, IT'S PRETTY LOUD IN THIS COCKPIT!
By Eisner Winners Art Baltazar & Franco
Titans in Space

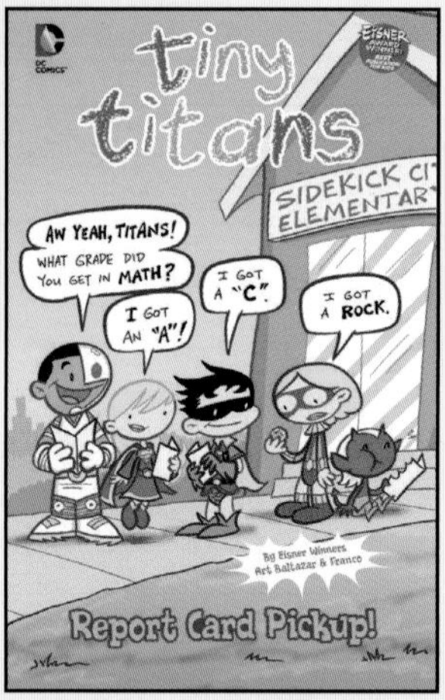
tiny titans
SIDEKICK CIT ELEMENTAR
AW YEAH, TITANS! WHAT GRADE DID YOU GET IN MATH?
I GOT AN "A"!
I GOT A "C".
I GOT A ROCK.
By Eisner Winners Art Baltazar & Franco
Report Card Pickup!

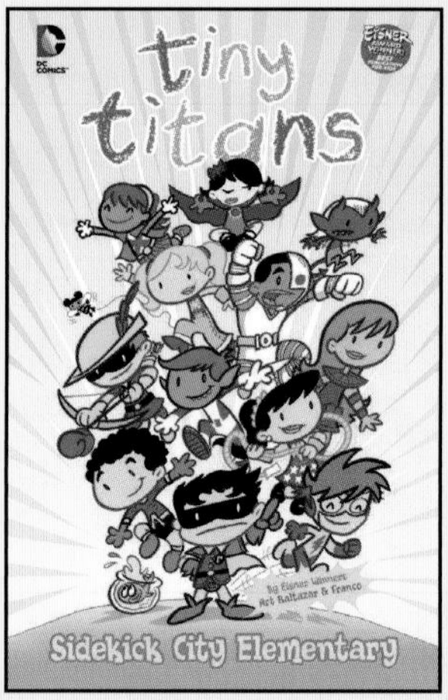
tiny titans
By Eisner Winners Art Baltazar & Franco
Sidekick City Elementary

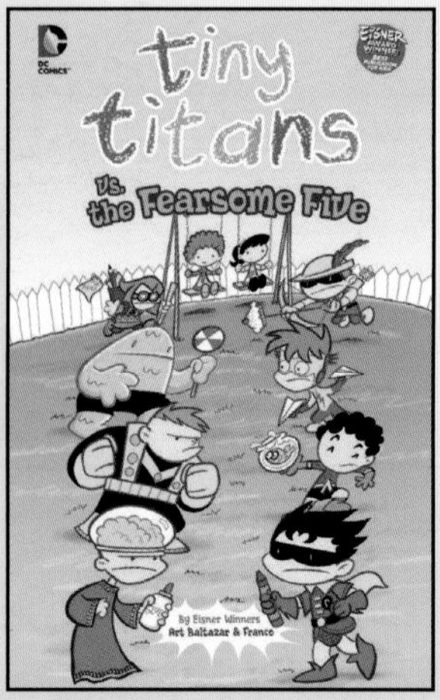
tiny titans
vs. the Fearsome Five
By Eisner Winners Art Baltazar & Franco

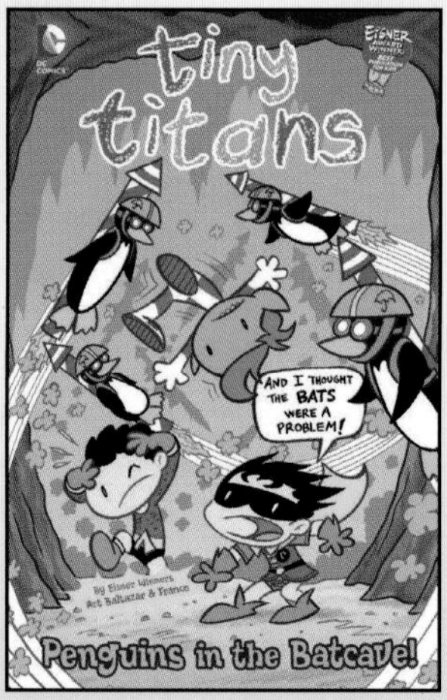
tiny titans
AND I THOUGHT THE BATS WERE A PROBLEM!
By Eisner Winners Art Baltazar & Franco
Penguins in the Batcave!

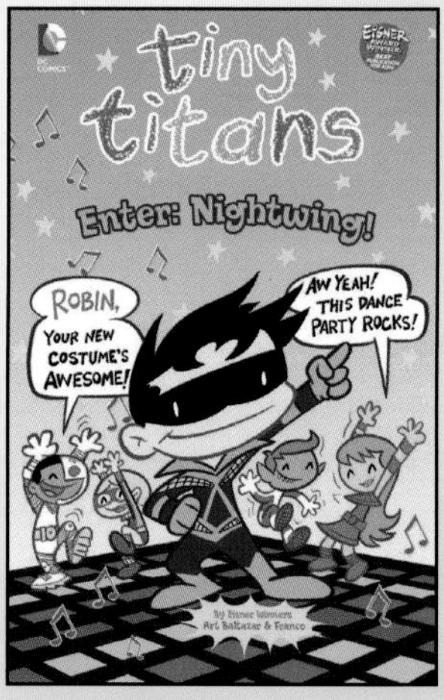
tiny titans
Enter: Nightwing!
ROBIN, YOUR NEW COSTUME'S AWESOME!
AW YEAH! THIS DANCE PARTY ROCKS!
By Eisner Winners Art Baltazar & Franco

FIND COOL WEBSITES AND MORE BOOKS LIKE THIS ONE AT WWW.FACTHOUND.COM.
JUST TYPE IN THE BOOK ID: 978-1-4342-4696-7